MW01145096

GIRL ALONE
ON AN ISLAND

SURVIVAL ISLAND SUSPENSE SERIES
BOOK TWO

A NOVEL BY
PAMELA LAUX MOLL

Girl Alone on an Island

A Novel by
Pamela Laux Moll

Copyright ©2016 by Pamela Laux Moll
First paperback edition © May2016
by Pamela Laux Moll

Printed in the United States of America
Book designed by Acepub
www.gopamela.com

ISBN: 978-1-892357-02-1
Beau Ridge Publishing

All rights reserved. No part of this book may be reproduced, scanned or distributed in any printed or electronic form without permission. Please do not participate in or encourage piracy of copyrighted materials in violation of the author's rights. Please purchase authorized editions.

This is a work of fiction. While, as in all fiction, the literary perceptions and insights are based on experiences, all names, characters, places, cruise lines, and incidents are either products of the author's imagination or are used fictitiously. No reference to any real person is intended or should be inferred.

In the Trilogy:

Island of Lies
Survival Island Suspense Series
Book One

∞∞∞∞∞∞∞∞∞∞

Girl Alone on an Island
Survival Island Suspense Series
Book Two

∞∞∞∞∞∞∞∞∞∞

Diamond Island
Survival Island Suspense Series
Book Three

∞∞∞∞∞∞∞∞∞∞

In memory of all the Treasure Hunters.

To my family

ACKNOWLEDGEMENTS

I am indebted to the following people for their contributions to this book. To my beta readers for their insights to making the story better: Jennifer Collins, Diane McPhearson, Debra Carlin, and Christine Nikles.

To all my family and friends for their encouragement and support that assisted me through the journey, from the bottom of my heart, thank you and to Kevin Carlin for the illustrations.

To my husband, Kyle, who stood by me through late hours and early mornings. To my kids, Lissa, Ben, Courtney, Tyler and Brandon.

PART I

RYLEIGH

*X marks the spot, with a dot, dot, dot and a
dash, dash, dash, and a big question mark.
Water running up, and water running down
and water running all around. A pinch and a
squeeze and a cool tropical breeze.*

Author Unknown

ONE

RYLEIGH, KEG KEY

ON THE FIFTH MORNING, Ryleigh sat cross-legged atop the platform in the tree, comparing the small islands all around her with the dots on the frail paper map that lay partially open across her lap. From where she squatted up on the lookout, suspended twenty feet above the beach, all she saw was a sea's worth of turquoise water flecked with lush green islands.

She was bare-chested and her ivory skin was baked brown under the constant, friendly Pacific sun. It was fall, but it didn't matter on the island. It was always summer there.

After the morning rain squalls, and with water still dripping from the thatched roof of her tiki hut home, Ryleigh had gotten a late start. Elevated on the plank, she huddled on the support built into the sturdy tall palm tree. The observatory, which was a few boards carelessly nailed to the crotch of a tree, was very well placed and in sight of the islands surrounding Keg Key. It had been built in haste last month by Elliot, when the pirate boats had been spotted off shore. Since then, she had added an equally careless array of rungs tacked to the trunk, almost close enough to provide access to the uncomfortable seat above.

She couldn't believe that in all of her thirty-two years as a Chicagoan, that she, Ryleigh Agatha Lane, would ever have found herself spending the last five days alone on a deserted island in the middle of nowhere – and, at times, wondering if Elliot, the person who'd left her there, would ever return to rescue her.

Even stranger to her, this wasn't her first week on the island, and it wasn't the first time she had come to the wooden perch in the palms. She'd climbed up to get a better view of the dumbbell shaped island in front of her, and the irony of her stranded situation made her feel like the dumbbell.

Her aerial view showed Brush Island to her left and Keg Key in the middle, with dozens of surrounding islands, for none of which she knew the names.

Sure, even Brush Island and Snake Island weren't their real names. Their real names, she couldn't pronounce.

"I have such a clear view to the tiki hut," she said. "My home for the last 38 days and nights. Some days, I think I'll go bananas living without the luxuries of civilization."

Elliot had lived alone here with her after the big storm. More than a month earlier, on a day excursion from the Royal Ahoy cruise liner, the ferry boats had returned to the ship before they could catch a ride back. They had been stranded together, with a few missed rescue attempts.

She'd only ever believed that you're born with one fate, and after she'd been brought into this world, she'd intended to grow up and live like her family did. A cozy house. Neighbors. Friends. Work. Play. But when someone named Elliot Finn took her on a cruise, and left her on an island, she was thrust into a lonely world of survival, hunger, and cavorting in the buff, totally without life's basic luxuries.

In her mind, she tried to deny his abandonment by ignoring the fact that he'd let her stay alone on the island, all for good reasons she knew, but still her subconscious harbored overwhelming grief. So much grief that she'd been violently ill for the first day. She missed Elliot terribly, and ached for him, but her destiny was set. She had a purpose in being there alone.

"I'll be down in a few minutes, Ebba," she yelled down to her white feral cat that was tantalizing a small lizard.

The faded, ink-sketched paper on her lap was the center of her attention. Every waking hour was spent studying the foreign dots and diagrams on the parchment, so much so that she had it memorized. She compared the tiny marks with the islands she saw to her left and to her right. The circles could be islands. Or they could not. There was one spherical shape on the map that looked like it had a tail. The smaller island to her right had a coral formation that jetted out of the sea on the tip of the island, and from her perch it looked like a tail.

"Hmmm. I never noticed that before. When standing on the water's edge, it doesn't appear to stick out of the water."

Ebba had chased a flying insect into the brush, but Ryleigh wasn't worried about the stray. She had always come back to the tiki hut beach. Ryleigh had heard about cats running away for six months, crossing three states and then returning home again.

It was through fate that the two had found each other. If she hadn't heard the purring that first night Elliot had left her on the island, she would probably have stayed in the tiki hut until he returned. Those first twenty-four hours alone had been miserable. A holy nightmare. There were no words to describe that huge heartache, sorrow, and the massive feeling of hopelessness. Then she'd found the cat.

The cat was a slender, beige and white, diminutive type that actually liked the water. Ryleigh had thought of naming her Minnow, because the white furry creature pawed at the small fish in the shallow surfs, but had instead called her Ebba after the tides.

"This dot next to the spherical one with the tail off to the left would be the brushy island where Elliot got us lost and we were stranded last month for a night." She often talked out loud – it helped her sanity at times.

"And this charcoal gray smudge running between brushy island and Keg Key is the boggy stream filled with snakes."

She felt excitement in the pit of her stomach, like the day she'd seen the two pirate boats show up on the island. She had been ecstatic that morning to see the ships and to know they would finally be rescued.

Things aren't always what they seem. The ships hadn't been friendly rescue boats. It turned out that the ships had been sent to the island by Dexco Pharmaceuticals, to make sure she never made it off the island alive.

"It's never that easy."

In the middle of the parchment paper, on the dumbbell-shaped splotch was a drawing of an image that looked like a barrel.

"A barrel? Wow, this isn't like a giant 'X' in the middle of the island."

It was significant. She knew it was. She felt it in her. "It's a symbol for where the treasure is hidden."

"Ebba!" she yelled. The cat came slinking back into sight. Ryleigh folded the map into quarters and tucked it under her faded bikini bottoms.

"It's going to be a good hunting day. The tides are low because it's almost a full moon." With the tides receding it left kilometers of ocean floor completely exposed and more areas of the sandy shoreline to explore.

Spinning on her bottom like a top, careful not to lose her balance, she felt a grin on her face, for the first time in a long time.

"Just my luck. This will be the right island with the treasures, and I'm left holding down the fort." She had the good sense to poke fun about her own predicament, to keep a positive attitude. The key to it all lay quietly waiting for her in these tropical islands.

She used the fronds as a ladder, carefully placing her calloused bare feet – with their fragments of pink, chipped nail polish on her toenails – on each protruding branch as she climbed down the tree until she reached the wood boards nailed at the base. When she got to the bottom of the palm's trunk, she picked up Ebba and nuzzled the cat close to her face.

"Maybe we can make use of this information. I'm pretty good with mysteries and puzzles. And we have nothing to do but wait for Elliot to return in seven days." She carried the white furball under her arm, until Ebba wiggled free, plopped down on all fours, and darted ahead of her on the path.

Ryleigh sidestepped a scurrying rat and shivered, despite knowing that it wouldn't hurt her. These weren't sewer rats like the ones found in the city. They were coconut rats. Vegetarians. Kinda cute, only a girl alone on an island would think.

A crackling sound snapped behind her. Ryleigh whipped around, in the direction of the noise and behind where the tree house palm stood, she saw a dark shadow in the brush.

Maybe another wild feral hog!

Panicked, but curious, she stared at the brush.

She stood frozen like a statue, barely breathing, mesmerized by the shape coming between rays of light. Her skin prickled.

If it was a hog, it was the biggest one yet.

TWO

THE SILHOUETTE IN the brush moved. She felt so impotent. *What would Elliot do?*

Ryleigh ran away from the palms and straight to the tiki hut for the knife. Her feet were accustomed to the path of crushed shells, rooted vines and sandy pot holes. Her breathing labored, her mouth dry, she felt anxious.

When she got to the hut, she threw open the door and ran to retrieve the knife. Strapping Elliot's knife to her waist with twine, reminded her of when he had hunted and killed a wild hog weeks earlier.

"Elliot. Why did you leave?" she called out to the empty tiki hut.

Something snapped in her head. All the loneliness, all the frustrations, all the loss bottled up inside of her was suddenly released. She pulled the knife out of the twine sheaf and threw it across the short distance to hit the side of the hut. It struck the dry wall and fell to the sandy planked floor.

"Perfect." She ran out of the hut and picked up a gallon-sized brown barrel. Carrying it over her head, she hurled it at the side of the rock fire pit. The decrepit but intriguing oak keg shattered open like a clear glass of water, the liquid contents exploding and spraying the rocks like diamond droplets.

With a loud cry of rage, Ryleigh ran down the beach – yelling and cursing, spinning around in the sand until she uncontrollably toppled to the ground, and curled up in a ball and rocked back and forth.

A lump gathered tight in her throat and she could feel the tears coming. She cried a lot these days since he'd left her. Sadness filled her tear covered face.

"Elliot! I'm sorry, I can't make it here without you. I can't kill a hog. I'm sorry. I've tried to accept my fate here. I really have tired," she said in a quieter voice.

"I can't accept that you left me here alone. You should be here with me," she said to the empty beach.

"Oh dear God," she said. "What am I going to do?"

Her breathing slowed as she straggled up and wiped the sand from her body. She looked out at the gray ocean, and saw the usual bordering islands as pinpoints all around her. They were like neighboring cities, so close but so far away.

She pulled out the map and gently unfolded it, then counting the dots as she held it up to the sky and matched the marks with the other islands across the sea. The feral hog, though, was not totally forgotten.

Two things she'd never thought she'd be hunting in her life – feral hogs and treasures.

THREE

ELLIOT

ELLIOT FINN RAN, chasing the helicopter. He shot three times at the cockpit. The chopper smoked and spun, out-of-control. He had hit the pilot!

"Shit!" he gasped under his breath. The whirling blades were falling toward him. He ran fast along the crushed shell path under his bloody feet, but it was too late. He yelled her name as he felt the vibrations of the blade as it dug into the sandy earth next to him, and the deadening sound as he dove into the sea–

The sheets were drenched. Again. Elliot took a long time to wake up, drifting in and out, aware that he was hot and wet.

Opening one eye, he looked over at the red digital numbers on the clock – 3:02 A.M. These last five days, he'd awakened earlier every morning and not been able to fall back to sleep. He turned over to stare at the empty spot in his bed, knowing that Ryleigh would be eating lunch about now. In another world, another hemisphere.

He felt a sting of guilt bite him every time he laid his head on the soft pillow and wrapped up in fresh, crisp linens. Most nights, he barely slept.

There was a brand new Louis Vuitton travel bag on the floor. Her bag. One he had neatly packed himself for her rescue. He had picked out and purchased every item –the prewashed denim jeans that the clerk had assured him were super-comfortable and would fit Ryleigh like a second skin, a blue gauzy top, a gray cashmere sweater, white panties, a lace bra, socks, converse tennis shoes, and fur-lined boots. He didn't know what footwear she would prefer to wear after going barefoot for so long. No longer would she need her flimsy sandals. The clothes would fit loosely because she would be thin. He had left her plenty of food for the ten days, but he knew she wouldn't eat much.

Five more days was the plan. After the pharmaceutical company trial, then he could rescue her. Would she take him back? They had lived apart, and he didn't like it, but it had given him a new perspective on life. He was tired of living for the moment, something he had done his whole life. He felt anxious to think that this woman could make him yearn for a future with her. He needed to see Ryleigh again, to be with her again. He ached for what they had become together.

Before he could force himself to fall back to sleep, his cell phone vibrated.

The text read, *come in.*

Crawling out of bed, he felt bleary-eyed and rattled by his haunting dreams. By 3:35, he was out of the shower and leaving his apartment.

His old reliable pickup truck was parked in the allotted spot under the covered and gated garage, but he bypassed it and chose the faster ride, his BMW M6. He jumped in the driver's side, clicked open the gate, and drove to the western edge of Tampa, a thirty-minute ride from his beach condo.

The humid air smelt of the gulf, reminding him of the island. The early morning birds' chirping reminded him of the seagulls on the island. He wondered if every smell and sound he noticed would remind him of the island, and of her being alone there.

A lot of things in his life reminded him of Ryleigh. And every thought of her dug deep into his soul.

He couldn't eat seafood since he had returned home and manged to avoid it. There were plenty of grouper sandwiches, tuna dips and fish entrees on the menus in Tampa. It wasn't that he couldn't stomach seafood after 33 days on Keg Key, it was that it conjured up images of Ryleigh. The way she looked dangling her bare feet off the black inner tube as he watched her attempt to fish for dinner, knowing perfectly well that she would end up throwing every single fish back into the ocean. If it hadn't been for Elliot, they might have starved. He was a survivalist.

As he high-wheeled it through the streets of his sleepy gulf town, Elliot remembered Ryleigh and the month long sojourn on the island, where he'd been infinitely content with her and the life they had made. He remembered every minute spent with Ryleigh – her emerald sea eyes, her mermaid silky hair, her warm smile. Her hopeful eyes, when he had promised her that he would never leave her there, and that it was only temporary.

"Please, promise me that if you can't come back–" her eyes had pleaded with tears on the edges.

"–Stop it, Ry. I will always come back, as planned."

"What if something happens to you?"

"I have back-ups. I'm not alone."

"Right. Your team," she said quietly, gently reminding him that she was a *mission*.

"You'll be just fine. This is the safest option. You have to hide here until the trial."

"I know. But my testimony? Without me there, how will you bring Dexco down?"

"Trust me. We have a plan," he said.

She nodded her head, so he continued. "Your testimony is set in five days. Then we will uncover the documents. There's a lot of arrests and other cover-ups being exposed."

"And you'll get your family back? Your brother and your two nieces?"

"Yes." There was a lot more to the plan that he couldn't share with her. No use making her worry. He knew her mental state had to be sharp for her to stay alone on an island for ten days, even if it was stocked with plenty of food, water, clothing and shelter. It wasn't her nutrition that he worried about; it was her mind.

She'd grown accustomed to the routines on the island, and they had both been happy with their temporary, stranded life together. Yes, it was her mind he worried the most about. Ryleigh had been living without all the modern conveniences, but it was the lack of human interaction that could drive anyone insane. No TV. No phones. No World Wide Web. No social media. Not another soul to interact with.

He hoped in his heart that by now the white, tamed cat he had left behind had found its way to her. That would help. He had wanted to leave a trained dog, that could swim, but that would have been too obvious. And who said cats don't like water? Elliot had made sure the one he'd left behind was an auburn and white Turkish Van breed, so called after Lake Van in Turkey where fable had it that this breed had been discovered to swim in the lake.

For whatever reason, he'd felt a furry companion would distract her from her stranded predicament. He worried that her sanity was like the ocean that surrounded her, and that her mind bobbed barely above the surface. After a month on the island, the passage of another week totally alone would be the seemingly unending test of his beautiful girlfriend's sanity.

He prayed she could stay sane for five more days.

FOUR

TAMPA REGIONAL HEADQUARTERS

ELLIOT USED HIS credentials at the front desk, and the older of the two guards said, "Go on up. They're expecting you."

"Thanks, Toby."

Elliot walked into the thirty-third floor conference room and saw that the director, and his closest friend, Dice – dressed in khaki pants, a designer pullover and blazer – sat at the head of the long table.

"Good morning, Elf." Dice used Elliot's nickname when he had bad news, figuring it would diminish Elliot's mood. But it had the opposite effect. He hated the name, and his stature was far from elf-like. Only the guys on his team knew his code name. It had started as a joke after his success on an assignment that had concluded on Christmas Eve. Coincidentally, it was his initials.

"You're up early, Dice. What's this about, that can't wait 'til the sun comes up?"

Dice didn't offer Elliot coffee. "There's trouble on the island."

Elliot, wearing a mask of non-concern over his face, but panicking inside, walked over to the long credenza and poured himself a cup of coffee. He held the pot up toward Dice. "Want a refresh?"

"No. Thanks."

"Dexco? Or the bird scientist?" Elliot knew that there would be an expedition to the island by a half-dozen scientists in thirty days, but he had planned to return for Ryleigh before then.

"No. Mother Fucking Nature." Dice turned his coffee cup to his lips, peering at Elliot over the top.

"What? Another storm?"

"No. An earthquake." Dice put his coffee down, and picked up some papers from his desk.

"What?" Elliot felt a strong feeling in the pit of his stomach. No, this couldn't be right. "Earthquakes can't be predicted."

"Exactly. Unless they're man-made to look like Mother Nature had a hand in them."

"A man-made earthquake?"

"It's top secret. A scientific experiment only known to a handful of agencies, including the CIA."

"I know meteorologists can study the movements of the atmosphere to forecast the weather." Elliot stared out the moonlit window. "And if you were here to tell me that the atmosphere is sending a tropical storm twisting toward the island, I would believe you. But come on, Dice, an earthquake?"

"Trust me, I didn't believe it either."

"How can that be? Scientists can make reasonably accurate long-term predictions when it comes to an earthquake location, but putting a precise timeframe on quakes is a bit more complicated, if not impossible."

Dice walked over to Elliot and handed him a thin stack of papers stapled at the side. "Look at this report... Puff the Magic Dragon. It's trouble."

"Puff? That's what this mission was about? Puff is the earthquake code name?" Elliot noticed a small blinking twitch in Dice's normally calm brown eyes. "Who's behind this? Are these government or corporate scientists?"

"I'm not sure whose payroll they're on. We do know there's a team of seismologists working the islands to the west, which includes all of the Keg Key atoll. They've been applying basic and scientific research to these islands. They're going forward with a seismic hazard assessment to predict the types of ground shaking expected from the earthquakes."

"In layman terms?"

"They're causing tremors."

"So, what does that do for the island?"

"They're going to cause explosions by injecting oils and gases into the core in that area. Their goal is examining the physics of the earthquake source and the propagation of seismic waves through the Earth's crust, and the local site's effects from it."

"Like reverse fracking." Elliot felt a lump forming in the back of his throat.

"Look, Elliot, there's no building structures on the island, so chances of anything falling and causing damage are slim. These are rupture scenarios they're looking at, and testing probable earthquake scenarios for specific faults with synthetic ground-motion injections."

"I'm not buying it. Why these islands? Why now?" The coffee's acid burned as it churned in his empty stomach.

"The ground beneath the atoll of islands, including Keg Key, has reached the breaking point. This is a good test site." Dice glanced at the papers he'd handed to Elliot. "It's all in the report. Underwater coral caves and the brown porous rock on top, both to the north and the south, have slowly squeezed Keg Key until the sandy crust holding it together can no longer stand the strain. With the scientists' help, in approximately seventy-two hours, the coral rocks could finally snap."

"Seventy-two hours? What the hell! What will happen to the island and the ones surrounding it?" He felt helpless, frustrated and angry.

"Calm down."

Elliot immediately fell into a chair facing the windows, the farthest away from the door. His stomach in knots.

"Scientists predict that if the coral shifts and snaps, it would cause erosion, slides, but no waves," Dice said.

"And what else?" Sweat beaded on Elliot's forehead.

"Well, if the action ended there, the slight readjustment of the ocean floor would result in a minor quake, registering no more than a magnitude of 4."

"Do these so-called adjustments happen a lot?" Elliot stood up and started pacing, not even realizing he had raised his voice to a shouting level.

"It has happened in the past, and the coral settlements on the ocean floor hit a tough patch of rock that merely slowed the fracturing down."

"But now?"

"Not this time. The force will make the cracks shoot up through the ocean crust, ultimately rupturing a circular path six miles across – with Keg Key as the epicenter."

"Oh God, no." Elliot wondered if he should go straight to the airport and go to her. He'd run out on a case once before. He could do it again. Take her away. Throw a dart on a map and just go there.

"Isn't the Ministry of Fisheries and Agricluture legally responsible for the management of all issues relating to the coral reefs and marine life? Can't we get to the foriegn diplomat there?"

"There's not enough time."

Elliot sighed heavily, closing his eyes for a moment. "Then my plans have changed. I can't complete this mission; I have–"

"–Stop, Elliot. Say no more. I don't want you to compromise your assignments or yourself."

"Fuck the plan. This is out of control." Maybe it was time to just get out. For the past few years, he had been almost constantly on the move, juggling his special missions while fighting the system. He wanted to settle down, with Ryleigh.

"Slow down. We'll modify the plan. Even if the scientists are right about the 72 hours, you would barely reach there in time without the military forces behind you. There's no way commercial transportation would ever get you there in time, and there's no one to communicate to locally that can make the rescue. At least not without jeopardizing the mission."

"Then we go to the top. Let's wake the President." Elliot reached for his cell phone and handed it to Dice.

FIVE
KEG KEY

RYLEIGH RIPPED a yellow strap off of a lawn chair that had been left behind by the cruise ship company. She wrapped the plastic binding around a skinny palm tree's trunk, tying it in a knot. Her hand brushed over the trunk, starting with the first yellow tie. "One. Two. Three. Four. And now five." Her eyes stung as she looked over her shoulder, out to the sea.

Today was the fifth day since Elliot had left her alone on the uninhabited island.

She grabbed the small notebook, found a place half-way through the pages, and wrote the date, and then in all caps she scribbled:

38!! DAY 38!

"First, I'm stranded here with my lover because of a tropical storm and a cruise ship excursion trip gone terribly wrong. Then, my *wonderful* lover hops on a helicopter and leaves me alone here for another ten days. And what's worse is I let him leave me here."

In the background, the high cliffs of the south side of the island towered, emerald green and brown while the sun showered twinkling light, like diamonds glittering across the ocean water.

Things aren't always what they seem.

She exhaled deeply and pushed a strand of her wet chestnut hair out of her eyes. She glanced over her shoulder and laughed at her wild island cat coming out of the jungle with a mouse between her teeth. "Come here, girl."

Ryleigh looked over her shoulder often, and feared nothing but the loneliness of the island. No speeding car had followed her to this part of the world. No black van had screeched up to the cruise ship landing to disgorge a pack of thugs to follow her onto the ship. She might feel completely and hopelessly trapped and alone here on the island, but she wasn't hunted day and night, like in Chicago. Well, not quite.

She murmured under her breath as she followed Ebba to the water. The cat must have heard her because it turned around and stretched its back.

Ryleigh knelt down and petted the underbelly of the mangy island cat. "I used to be a nice, happy person, Ebba. Really, I was. Just last year, I was the kinda girl that would never have survived a month and a half isolated on a deserted island. I was nice to be around, too."

Hopefully, somewhere deep inside, she was still nice, but she'd taken so many brutal blows in the past few months that Ryleigh couldn't feel anything but the dull pain of the layered bruises.

Elliot had laid out a new life plan for her. One thing was clear, though – she wasn't a hundred percent convinced that their two plans aligned. One day, she thought, one day soon, she would be able to share her plans for her life with him.

"Let's eat dinner, Ebba. I've got some treasure hunting to do tomorrow. Wouldn't Elliot be surprised if he came back in five days and I had actually solved a mysterious legend?"

The night air was full of sea salt and promise.

She wondered if Elliot believed in pirates and hidden treasures. Did she?

What else did she have to do while waiting for Elliot to return to rescue her?

Ryleigh sat on a lawn chair, unwrapped a few palm leaves stored near the fire pit, and scooped up with her fingers a few small pieces of fish from the leaves. She put them in her mouth, not even tasting the salty dried fish she had smoked the day before. Ebba jumped on her lap, startling her.

"Sorry, girl, where's my manners?" She unwrapped another leaf and laid it on the sand. Ebba jumped off of her lap and greedily ate the fish.

"What would I do without you? I would probably still be locked in the tiki hut, afraid to come out, and not caring whether I lived or not."

The cat looked up at her, with one big green eye and one blue, and then fell to its side and licked its paws.

"Yep, Ebba, you're the reason to get up every day. I thank God I found you the day after he abandoned me here."

Ryleigh heard a rustle behind her in the brush. Ebba sat up, hearing it, too.

"Not the hog again." She needed to go after the boar, and hunt it like Elliot had done several times before. He had been successful on one of his hunting trips. "The meat was so good, Ebba."

She looked to the sky and saw the sun lowering itself down to the west – almost time for another beautiful island sunset. Alone. How many times had her life recently been single-handing? She clasped her hands firmly in her lap, and resisted an overwhelming urge to run to the tent for the map again. Instead, she sat stiffly on the worn lawn chair while Ebba sat at her feet, watchful and protective.

"It's almost dark, and there's no reason to hunt at dusk. Let's get a good night's sleep and look for the boar tomorrow, and, who knows – maybe try and interpret this map."

She now knew how Tom Hanks had felt in *Castaway*. He'd spent a lot of time talking to a volleyball named Wilson. As if the cat read her mind, it jumped on her chest and brushed its back against her face. "Well, at least Wilson didn't need to be fed. I know you're hungry, Ebba, but I don't feel like fishing tonight, and that's all the fish we have."

A few minutes later, Ryleigh took off her tattered blue shirt and lay down on the hard hut floor. Unable to sleep, she wondered how the last few weeks' horrible events could have pushed her farther and farther from the man who she in fact loved.

She followed the palm's branches, crisscrossing the ceiling with her eyes, trying to think, to let her embers reacquaint themselves with Elliot's sexiness and manly curves. What the hell was she thinking? Why was she so worried about this, when there was so much else to worry about?

She stood up and pulled the thatched door tightly closed, and wrapped a twine around the knob. It wouldn't stop a monstrous pirate sneaking in to slit her throat at night, but it did keep the wind from blowing the door wide open. Ebba curled up by her head. She hugged the cat.

"Nightie night, Eb."

She turned off the flashlight.

SIX

THE NIGHTS WERE the worst. She slept uneasily and always felt disturbed. Alone with her thoughts and the strong ache for Elliot to be at her side. No matter how much she felt he had betrayed her to save his family, and to save her, he said, she missed him, and wondered if she would still love him when he returned.

At night, she was always afraid. It was as if Elliot's absence had awakened something inside of her. Something that made her constantly feel like she wasn't alone on the island. A scary feeling inside her.

Even the beach looked calm and serene during the day. Whenever she stood on the beach at night, it was a scary sight. The waves roaring and hitting the shore in pitch dark. The sea instilled awe and wonder, but also filled fear into her.

A few hours after turning out her light, she was still staring into the dark. Nights like this, she missed Elliot, she missed a glass of wine, and she missed sleeping pills.

Not five feet away, just on the other side of the thatched wall, was the carbon black surf, and the night and the jungle. Ryleigh lay in the dark most nights in fear. The island was empty, and she knew this. She'd been all over the island and there was no sign of other human life, anywhere. She wasn't afraid of the island animals. Her tiki hut protected her from wild creatures and storms. On really bad storm days, she had caves to hide in. But at night she was afraid.

On nights when there was no moon, it was utterly dark. She'd opened her eyes wide. She would hold her hand in front of her face, but she couldn't even see it.

When the ocean breezes were blowing like they were now, she heard new sounds. Her imaginings of what was waiting outside the hut made her hair stand up. The nights had been the worst, and her imaginative mind moved her to the rim of sheer island madness.

She had a few flashlights, including the underwater one. She didn't want Elliot to come back for her and find the flashlights were out of batteries. But what would Elliot care about more – a working flashlight or a girlfriend that had gone mad?

She turned on the flashlight. She saw nothing out of place in her home, the tiki hut. As she lay on the floor, she stared at the thatched ceiling above her. She pulled the quilt she had made out of cruise ship t-shirts over her legs, pointing the flashlight beam over the colorful quilt. Jersey fabrics of colorful slogans – *What happens on the ship stays on the ship, I love big boats, I heart Cruises* – and there were plenty of *Captain* and *Sailor* shirts, too. The blanket was patchy and irregular, made from mostly children's and small adult's shirts. The L, XL and XLL shirts, she wore like dresses. Her favorites had used to be the simple slogans or the ones with the big anchor on the front. And, most days, she wore the plain white t-shirts that had no slogan, with only her fraying swimsuit bottoms or a sheath. She didn't want to encounter a wild pirate someday and have to fight for her life or negotiate a way off the island wearing a t-shirt that said, *Ship faced.*

Food, water and shelter had all been provided before Elliot left. And clothing was important, too. It protected her from bugs and the blazing sun, even though the tiki hut was abundantly stocked with insect sprays and sunscreens.

Had these items really been left behind by accident? Or had Elliot stocked the supplies? Like he had the large knife she used for hunting and fileting fish? And the port-a-potties. There were several left behind. But most days, she went in the woods and dug a deep hole, and did her business in the hole. She buried the tissue paper and left no signs of it behind. Elliot had taught her many wilderness survival techniques.

But he hadn't been able to get inside her head. He'd tired. He'd tried to teach her to meditate through the darkness at nights, through the loneliness, through the boredom. She would try, for Elliot, not to go mad before he returned.

She turned off the flashlight.

She turned it back on. Then off. Then on.

It might have been another hour before she fell asleep. Ryleigh slept, but she tossed and turned and awakened several times throughout the night. She dreamt that Elliot was lying next to her. "I told you I'd be back. I told you I'd be here for you." His image whispered in her ear. She knew she would see Elliot hundreds, thousands of times in her sleep.

Elliot's image disappeared.

She dreamt of a giant boar shadow figure rising over the tiki hut, and of snakes and seaweed monsters rising out of the ocean and reaching up and grabbing Elliot's helicopter out of the sky.

"No!" she yelled, and sat up in bed. Ebba was snoring, curled up on a pile of cruise ship t-shirts in the corner of the hut. She lay back down and slept with one eye open until nearly dawn.

She felt better the next morning. The tiki hut was undisturbed, and she laughed at herself for the absurdity of her dreams. "I will not let these next five days here turn me into 'Here's Johnny' in the movie *The Shining*." The movie had bothered her when she'd first seen it. Sometimes, she now knew how an isolated innkeeper stuck inside for the winter had kept imagining the motel was haunted.

She stretched and took off the large, warm t-shirt she wore every night as a nightgown. Ryleigh searched the stack of souvenir t-shirts, and chose a bright orange one. She put it on and, before she slipped out of the tiki hut, she noticed that the twine wrapped around the makeshift handles was undone, and that the door was ajar, Ebba gone.

"How did that happen?"

She made a mental note to tie a tighter knot that night.

SEVEN

WITHIN THE LAST FEW hours, a glowing orange South Pacific sun had slowly peeked over the horizon and begun to first warm and then, morphing to an eye-burning yellow, bake the sand and everything below it. Ryleigh completed her daily chores like a woman possessed.

Little chores on the island were how Ryleigh hid from her thoughts. She filled the water pots from the desalinization station. She threw a few hard-grained coconut shells on the fire like charcoal. When it was burning well, she set up a skewer of whelk conch to roast and filled another pot with coconut milk. She gathered her night t-shirt, shook it, and hung it on the lawnchair to air.

Making the bed in the tiki hut took five seconds. It was important to keep some resemblance to life back home, which included these daily chores and personal hygiene.

A paper rustled under the pillow. Had she accidentally left the worn map under the makeshift pillow? It fluttered in the island breeze as Ryleigh pulled the pillow off the ground. Before returning it to the tiny dirt safe under the plank floor, she scanned the map twice, checking every mark on it.

These were the habits of a former document control director. 'Former' because she was pretty sure by that now she had been fired from her job at Dexco Pharmaceuticals. She had been a no-show from work for weeks now. But then, someone at Dexco already knew that she'd never return to work, because they wanted her dead.

"I am considered dead by now. If Elliot does his job right. I'm dead. Shark bait. Buried at sea."

She left the hut and finished preparing breakfast.

"My life has been one fickle, messed-up bitch," she said to her island cat, as she made the boiling coconut juice mixture, her version of morning coffee since the third day of having been stuck on the island.

"At least the cruise chefs of the tiki hut or Elliot could have left me coffee." Her hand shook as she held the tin cup.

The sadness that she had kept tampered down since she'd learned about Elliot's betrayal, his hand in their stranded state, and his abandonment – even when he'd said he cared deeply for her and that he had to leave her there to protect her and his family – erupted again.

"Yeah, maybe I made it too damn easy for him. It was true that I had little choice, and most of them ended with my death, but to have the blood of others on my hands. I couldn't do it."

She picked up the cat and nuzzled her cheek against its head, and closed her eyes. The anxious meows that accompanied the purring noise told her that Ebba expected breakfast.

She put the cat down. "What did you do before I rescued you? Have you gotten lazy? Not wanting to find your own food?

"You know I hate cats, don't you? I'm not a cat person. I love dogs."

She ate a small helping of fresh fruits sprinkled with shaved coconut.

Maybe Elliot hadn't been responsible for some of the items she had found while exploring. Maybe there were fishing expeditions to the island, and so far it was an off-season. Maybe someone would just sail up one morning and walk onto the beach and ask to camp with her. "With all these 'maybes', this is why I wake up every morning, Ebba. There's hope. Some hope."

She stood up and looked out at the cold blue sea. "You know, looking at this view every morning never gets old. I could probably just give it all up, give up my life back in Chicago and live here," she said. "Oh yeah, I already did."

She strolled to the tiki hut. During her sojourn on the tiny island, a yellow notebook had become her diary. Opening it now, she wrote, *Day 39*. She never added the date in the morning, since the day had just begun, and there was still plenty of time to get rescued or die. Sometimes, she thought, living here alone was far harder than dying.

For the first few days after Elliot left, she hadn't left the tiki hut beach area; instead she'd gone for long swims in high waves until she was exhausted. Ryleigh had thought then that that might be the day she died.

How the hell did I let this happen? She hadn't let this happen. Her company had caused this. And what had happened afterward? She clenched her jaw, grinding her teeth. She was only human. And what happened next? Her falling in love with Elliot. She had let that happen. The lies they'd told each other. And now everything was an elaborately staged plan to force her to be stranded away from testifying against her employer in the most publicized trial in pharmaceutical history. But how would they be exposed without her there? That part of the plan, Elliot had never shared with her.

In a few days, the trial back home would come to a crescendo. Dexco would be exposed, and justice would be served. The price for now, her freedom.

EIGHT

COOK COUNTY PRECINCT STATION

WITH A LOT of effort, Detective Joe Chandler tried unsuccessfully to pace the holding area of the largest precinct in Chicago. He nodded his head at a bonds man, "Controlled chaos."

Ricardo frowned back at him.

Chandler saw the hallways overflowing with prisoners beginning their due process in the county lockup. Pacing back and forth, he scanned the hectic small room, looking for a particular informant.

A man wearing a faded Tommy Bahama Hawaiian shirt, blue jean shorts, and a pair of lace-up, tan boat shoes, one shoe untied and a shiner on his left eye, looked out-of-place in a Chicago jail in the fall.

"Can you move that one to an interview room?" Chandler asked the officer in the hallway.

Chandler entered the small room, highly motivated and dedicated to this case, and extended his hand to the prisoner and introduced himself, "I'm Detective Chandler. Thank you for cooperating."

"That was my deal, detective," the prisoner said.

"Ah, good. That makes this conversation easy," Chandler replied. "Who did the lady work for at the pharmaceutical company?"

The man across the table went from being calm to nervous once the questioning started.

"The girl? I worked a small gig last night, on a yacht."

"Of course you did," Chandler knew that from the briefing file. His disgust for the snitch showed in his sarcastic reply. He had never met an informant that wouldn't give up information to save himself from some other petty crimes he'd committed in getting the information. "Is that where you got in the fight?" Chandler pointed toward the black eye.

"I worked as a valet at the dock. My job was to park the cars and watch the other boats while they sailed. I got in a shuffle with another valet that took my tips at the end of the night."

"Did you hear anything on board the yacht or while parking the cars, about the girl?" Chandler jotted notes on a small spiral pad and didn't look up at the informant. He didn't need to. He saw the man hesitate, which meant he knew something, and he wanted something back in exchange.

"What about my arrest?" He pointed to his left eye.

"Aw, here you go, already." Chandler picked up the file on the table in front of him. He read the first few paragraphs.

"Well, we're gonna dismiss the one-four-eight…"

"Okay."

"And you'd plea to the six-four-seven, if– "Chandler waited for his reaction to the plea on the disorderly conduct, rather than the charge he was giving up on the resisting arrest.

"Yeah, well, what do need from me? I usually go along with what Elliot says."

"Elliot?" Chandler wasn't aware of the detective. "City cop? Or attorney?"

"No... Wait, who sent you?" He looked frustrated by this change in the conversation with the detective.

"I'm not here specifically working the pharmaceutical trial case. I'm interested in the girl that worked there because she had a friend on a cruise that went missing." Chandler would need to know more about Elliot. "Wasn't he the other passenger?"

"Look, I don't know anything about a cruise ship."

"Tell me what you do know, and I can make these charges go away, even the resisting and disorderly." The interview had gone from on-track to a totally fucked-up mess. Why Elliot? Didn't this guy have information about the missing girl from the Ahoy Cruise ship accident he was investigating? So far, no one had noticed whether the young manager, Ryleigh Lane, had or had not returned from her cruise. And he was investigating why. He owed some dead people that much.

"I was hired to find out about a guy's girlfriend. She works for the pharmaceutical company that had the party last night on Lake Michigan." He stopped and looked at the clock again. "Can I get some coffee? It was a long night in holding."

"Yay, I could use some, too," Chandler said. He knocked on the window. A deputy, fair-skinned and freckled and with wavy red hair, came to the door. "Can we get two cups of coffee?"

"Sugar and milk?" the informant asked.

"Make one black, and one foo-foo." He smiled at the deputy and winked.

"Don't guess I can get a cig, too?"

"No. Not happening now." Chandler opened the file. "Did I see they found possession of cocaine?"

"What!" The informant jumped up, knocking his chair over in the process. "That's blackmail. I don't use. Everyone knows that. I drink a lot of whiskey and chase the skirts, but I don't use."

"I didn't say it was yours. I see where one of the Cadillacs you parked, when you got out of the car, three small plastic baggies of cocaine – that maybe you intended to sell to the guests – fell to the ground near the officer's feet. The baggies were in plain view of law enforcement and are impounded as evidence."

"What? That wasn't mine."

"Further search, police found secret compartments within the caddie interior. Some type of solenoid-activated partitions were discovered in the backseat on the driver's side. One-and-a-half kilos of cocaine and some cash were found in the concealed hiding places."

"I didn't even park a caddie all night."

"Are you sure?"

"Yeah, I'm sure. There were a lot of Jags, Ferraris, one Ashton Martin, Porsches... this wasn't a caddie crowd. Someone's being set up."

The deputy returned with two cups of coffee. Chandler took a sip of the hot black liquid. And the man across the table did the same from his cup.

"Okay, let's just say someone at the party wanted you or another valet to take the dive on the drugs and money. Why? What do you know?"

"I know nothing about the coke and money. This was supposed to be about a girlfriend."

"Elliot's?"

The informant looked toward the small window on the door. "Yeah."

"Yeah, but what? You don't really think the pharmaceutical broad is his girlfriend, do you?" Chandler had known an Elliot once, at the CIA office out of Tampa. Seeing as the cruise ship incident had taken place in international waters, the FBI couldn't do much, but the CIA could.

"Look, I was paid to find out information at the yacht party, or anything I could get out of the passengers."

"Did he have one in particular in mind?"

"Passengers?"

"Yeah."

He shifted in his chair, staring at his hands before picking up his coffee again. He took a swallow, and set the cup down. "If I tell you which car, you drop all charges?"

"If you don't tell me, I will turn all this material over to the FBI. They're interested in the cocaine caddie."

The informant squirmed in his chair.

Chandler looked at the file. "Look, I'm not asking for much info from you, and I can get what I need one way or another. There were only a handful of cars, and there's footage from traffic cameras at the corner and the yacht club has cameras. The drug rap is bogus, so charges will never be filed unless I give the FBI due cause."

"Okay. One of the valets knows Elliot, and he got me the job. I made double money for the night – my tips, the job, and the surveillance. I just wanted my tips back, and didn't mean to break the guy's nose."

"He'll live. Screw the tips, too – not worth another night in lockup. We'll drop the charges. Now, whose vehicle were you watching?"

"The President of Dexco. Man, he has a sweet ride; a red Ferrari."

NINE

PUZZLED, CHANDLER felt his brow crease. "Did you bug it?"

"You bet I did. He was with a girl he called Anna. And she, well, she started kissing all over the guy as he drove. Then she had her way with him while he was driving down Lake Shore Drive at Navy Pier, and he was done before he got to Millennium Park." He sported a gummy grin that showcased bad veneers.

"Stop fantazing. Then what happened?"

"He dropped the chick off at that little boutique hotel across from the Hilton."

"The Blackstone?"

"Yup, then he went to another chick's house. And he did all this before his wife even got her limo ride back to their house in Naperville."

"He stayed in the city?"

The informant nodded. "At his condo in Trump Tower."

"Okay. Why do you think Elliot paid you for information on Greg Edersom?"

"Beats me. The guy is super-rich, and I just figured one of his play pals is Elliot's girlfriend. I'm not into all this other politics."

"Seems Elliot went to a lot of trouble just to catch his girl cheating."

"I see all types."

"What else did you hear? Can I hear the recording?"

"No, I listen in through my receiver, made a zipped audio file and put it on a memory stick. Hid it at the boat dock for Elliot to retrieve it later."

"You did all this while working too?"

"Yeah. I'm good at what I do. As soon as the guy and his bimbo left, I listened in and later hid the memory drive."

"Before your fight? And your resisting arrest?" Chandler wanted to remind him who was controlling the Get-out-of-Jail-Free card.

"Yeah. Elliot has it all by now. The Dexco dude made one call after he dropped off the chick."

"His wife?"

"No. A scientist."

"A what?"

"I heard him talking about gases and explosions, and the guy on the other end of the speaker phone sounded very geeky. I didn't understand half the words he used."

"Try me?" Chandler knew the pharmaceutical company had a lot of scientists on staff.

"Something about a sampling of some kind of research for some islands, some intergalactic earthquake."

"Earthquake? You sure you heard them right?"

"Yup, I'm sure. Maybe it's a code name? Because the way they talked, they made it sound like it was a party they were going to on a set date. Like you can plan an earthquake." The informant shook his head in disbelief.

Chandler didn't blink. He merely said, "I'm not sure I heard you right."

"No, you heard me right."

Chandler rubbed the five o'clock shadow of whiskers on his chin.

"I'm sure as shit that's what he said. He even went on to say that if there was an earthquake on the island, and it killed all its inhabitants, that would be a beautiful thing. Everyone could be buried. Secrets and treasures stay buried." He took a sip of coffee and shifted in his chair.

"Secrets and treasures? This is goddamn crazy."

There was a silence. The informant waited for Chandler to understand. Perplexed, he just scratched his head. "I don't get it."

The Hawaii-clad man nodded.

The loquacious informant kept talking about the earthquakes giving information to Chandler he hadn't heard before.

"I'll bet you a dozen doughnuts, copper, that they are up to something on those islands." "Did they mention a location?" Chandler asked.

"It's funny you ask that. He mentioned some islands that I ain't ever heard of."

Which was probably ninety percent of the world's geography, Chandler thought. "Any specific names you remember?"

"Yeah. I do. It reminded me of a fraternity party. Keg Island." The informant looked proud of his astute memory.

Chandler had heard of that island. "Wait a minute," he said aloud. That had been one of the excursions on the last Royal Ahoy Line cruise stops.

Maybe it was time for a vacation. Chandler would have his clients pay for a trip to Keg Island, where he could have a look around. He'd leave tomorrow morning, right after he checked out the red Ferrari's owner.

TEN

DAY 39

AFTER BREAKFAST, Ryleigh followed the furthest path to the east. The map tucked in her worn leather belt next to her knife opposite of the water bottle, making her feel like a poseur cowgirl.

"What will be there when I find the right location? And what are the odds? I'm here on some unchartered island out in the middle of the sea, and there may be a hidden treasure that was left here centuries ago. Even if I do find it, then what? Who cares if I find innumerable tons of gold or chests full of diamonds and jewels?"

The map was a puzzle, a welcome challenge, and she was equal to it. A girl free here to do... just about anything. The possibilities of the place seemed to unfold endlessly.

She needed to find the treasure, just like she'd needed to find herself all these years, living alone. She had to hunt to save, or at least to find, her sanity.

It was sometimes hard for her to believe that, just a month and a half ago, the Royal Ahoy Cruise ship had dropped off a ferry full of passengers to this very island for a day's excursion at the beach. "That turned out well," she said. "If only Elliot and I hadn't taken off to find a private place just minutes after the ferry dropped anchor."

She often wondered what Elliot was doing back home. Had he exposed Dexco yet?

Ominous clouds rolled by and seagulls circling overhead squawked at her like it was a warning. She loved the beautiful island, but sometimes she felt like she was being watched.

Yet, there she was on this luminous afternoon, searching for both a victory in her soul and a material one. Wearing a mask of concern, she moved sluggishly through the fields, feeling the calluses and blisters on her heels from the long walks all over the island. Most days, she didn't wear anything on her feet. Today, she wore modified flip-flops, the source of most of her blisters, but Band-Aids from the tiki hut covered both feet like sticky, beige war badges.

"Am I sure this is the way?" She generally had a good sense of direction – in the city. In many ways, though, the streets of Chicago were easier to navigate than the jungle paths.

She and Elliot had been to this side of the island once, and the trip had been a long hike, but the rewards were indescribable.

Why hadn't the cruise ship come back? Didn't they want to take their supplies? Wouldn't they be surprised to find a mess of the tiki hut? And to find her? Elliot had told her the cruise ship had been sold to another company and that the new owners didn't plan to sail to Keg Key. But wouldn't they eventually come back?

During their first week stranded, they had first come to this side of the island. They had walked a few steps hand-in-hand until their pathway became too narrow for them to walk alongside each other.

"I loved that day." She remembered following behind Elliot and studying him from the back side. Remembering that day, how it had felt like a honeymoon with her new lover, she knew now it had been no honeymoon. *Elliot, mystery man, Hunk-berry, Elliot. Who are you?* Kind of like a Rambo, which she had thought was hot.

They had stopped at the top of the hill and sat upon a flat rock. He had wrapped a strong, tanned arm around her midsection, where the small t-shirt was tied up. He had said, "I want today to be special. I want you to be focused on this trip."

"Okay, I'm focused. I don't see what the big deal is. You're always showing me the trails and directions."

"But this way is different, you'll see," he had said with excitement in his voice.

She had watched Elliot as he continued down the rugged trail. The crystal blue sky peeking through the trees now and then, and a glimpse of the sapphire ocean everywhere they looked.

When they had reached the top, and the turning point toward the descent to the other side, they'd stood and looked out. It had taken her breath away.

From the very top of the north side, the tall, skinny palm trees and mangroves stopped short of a field of pink bougainvillea and blood red hibiscus, that congealed into a tropical vista.

Amid the thick brush of the mangroves, a storied flock of seagulls, cranes, and pink flamingo birds peppered the brush.

Elliot had stood next to her, both of their breathing patterns rhythmic from climbing the hill, and from the majestic views.

"Beautiful." She said it now, and had back then.

Ryleigh removed the plastic water bottle from her waist where it dangled, and brought it to her lips without ever looking at it, keeping her eyes on the landscape. She took one more swig of the water, retied it, and continued down the hill.

Ten minutes later, she stopped, resting in the middle of the flower hill and drank more water. The breeze blowing off the hillside was sweet with flowers and salt.

Ryleigh believed in buried treasures. It was real to her. There were the odd symbols that resembled kegs of whiskey. She had heard the island had been nicknamed Keg Key after the kegs of beers brought over from the cruise ship excursions.

"But, what if the pirates made whiskey or wine here? And what happed to all the old kegs? Did they trade the whiskey for treasures? Or could this just be a map to the place they made the whiskey?"

She turned the paper over. Nothing to show its authenticity. But she knew it was real. "If it's a treasure map, where's the giant 'X' that marks the spot of the gold?"

Just like her childhood song. Her parents would draw with their fingers on hers and Caleigh's backs, and sing a song: X marks the spot (And they would trace an "X" on their backs), with a dot, dot, dot (with the same finger, they would lightly poke three dots on their backs), and a dash, dash, dash (they'd trace three horizontal dashes, one below the other), and a big question mark (tracing a big question mark). And a pinch and a squeeze (and they would pinch and squeeze them) and a cool tropical breeze.... (they would blow on their backs).

The girls would giggle from the pinches and the squeezes. Whenever Caleigh tried to repeat the song and draw on Ryleigh's back, she couldn't pronounce "and a cool tropical breeze." Caleigh would blow and mumble a strange sound instead.

The song had been modified to accommodate Caleigh's speech impediment, and instead of singing, a pinch and a squeeze and a cool tropical breeze, the lines were replaced with, water trickles up (with both hands, they would move their fingers upwards) and water trickles down (they'd run their hands down) and water trickles all around. Crack! They would pretend to crack an egg over the twins' heads by knocking their knuckles together. Then, they'd pretend to let egg cascade downward by lightly touching their heads with their fingers.

Ryleigh laughed and folded the paper back in half, and as she did she noticed that the two halves – when folded – formed an oval circle, like an egg.

She peered through the loosely woven, yellow cotton bandana that covered her forehead, and examined the hillside. The stop-you-in-your-tracks electrifying pink of the beautiful flowering field of bougainvillea had been her favorite place of those she and Elliot would visit. It was a good hour hike from the tiki hut camp site, and another two hours to the other side, where the caves and rocky coral shore smelled like dead seaweed.

The map had been folded so many times over that the square corners where the paper had been crunched together, left small lines on the fine paper.

The markings were almost caveman like. Not typewritten, and definitely not English. The ink looked like it had been written with a calligraphy pen, like the ones used in wedding invitations. The ink had smudged in places where it hadn't dried before being folded.

She held up the map, folded length-wise, and the random rocks, trees, and bushes now became more pronounced. "This is a circle of tightly clustered bushes, flowering bushes."

She felt excitement inside her, like she had a purpose. "Oh my, this is crazy. Or maybe I'm just crazy. But the plants on the folded map look like the bushes in flowering mode; yet, when I open the paper, it looks like a different hill."

The smell of the aromatic flowers was particularly invigorating. She sat down again and laid her head flat on the hill. She remembered when Elliot had kissed her that day they'd first come there. They'd been tired, confused, experiencing mixed emotions about each other, and yet it had been so romantic.

She held the paper up, letting the slanted sun rays pierce through the thin paper. "The dots, here and there, not trees, maybe stars." Her dad had taught her how to read stars. He'd said she could map the world through the stars.

"Oh, where are you, Elliot?"

It was amazing how, even now, after he had left her alone on the island, abandoning her, she constantly thought about him, and only him. "How could you have left me here?"

But this amazing island had been the perfect surroundings for him to further attempt to seduce her into the plan they had made. Elliot had known these surroundings would be perfect. Didn't all women love all that romanticism? Beautiful, sandy white beaches, crystal blue waters, fields of colorful flowers? Elliot had romanticized everything only until he had accomplished his objective.

Elliot had been like a savior to her all that month, stranded alone.

"Wait a minute." She had to remind herself, he had planned it. Hunk-a-Elliot Finn had probably never had to pursue women. They'd probably chased after him. She should have known, with so many women chasing after him... what was he doing chasing after her?

A few days ago, had been her first few days here alone without him. It had been hell. She remembered floating on her back the second day, with her arms over her head. She'd laid there listlessly, with barely her head above the water, aware that an undertow could carry her out to sea. A current had come up and swept her along, parallel to the beach. She'd thought about laying there and seeing where the sea took her. She really hadn't cared. She had thought she should just float away, but she wasn't ready to leave Keg Key, yet. That day had not been her day to die.

She jumped up and turned toward the half circle of lily flowers. "Why does the keg symbol end there?"

She had nothing but time. She would go and see.

ELEVEN

INTRIGUED, RYLEIGH quickened her pace and, after twenty minutes, and maybe a mile's distance across the hill, when she arrived at the area that looked to have the mark of a keg, she realized there was a brook running behind the trees.

She smiled pleasantly. "Wow, water!" Had Elliot found this? Ryleigh assessed her surroundings for a minute. Suddenly, a cool tropical breeze kicked up and actually, for the first time on the island, she felt a bit chilly, and she hugged herself.

"This is a fabulous place," she said. She took off her flip-flops and dipped her toes into the smooth, cool water. "A fresh spring?" She knelt down and dipped a few fingers in the water, and smelled it. Clear, crisp. She touched her fingers to her lips.

"No salt."

She inspected the water's source, to the extent that she could see it, and saw the brook ran right up to the caves from a large pool. "It's such a peaceful place." The sound of the currents hugging the rocks along the cave edges made for an unspoiled place to relax on a warm, lazy afternoon. "So, this is the treasure? Water. Fresh water?"

And it was very romantic. Her insides ached for Elliot, for his touch, for his strong arms around her.

She took out her bottle and finished drinking the last of the sterilized water, then filled the empty plastic bottle with the lagoon water. "I'll purify this when I get back to camp." She wasn't suspicious of the water, but she wanted to be sure. She couldn't afford to get sick. Not here, alone. She knew that the water could look extremely clear and healthy, but still have foreign bacteria in it. At least she didn't have to worry about pesticides or chemical run-offs. Not here.

"But a clean bath in non-salty water is appropriate." Since they had lived on the island together, they had managed to ration their water to a few gallons a day each. Take away flushing toilets, and running showers, and they could live on five gallons of water a day. Anything less and they would start feeling lethargic from dehydration, food contamination, and lack of personal hygiene.

With her t-shirt and bathing suit bottoms tossed aside, she dove into the cold, crystal clear water. "Oh my God!" she yelled when she came up for air. "So cold!"

She swam in the deep water, which got deeper as she neared the caves. When she was in water over her shoulders, she stood and examined a small waterfall. "Was that on the map?" She swam closer. Her mane of wet, matted brown hair hung like twisted ropes down her back.

The water spilled from a lip of the stream, pooling into a basin. She went underwater and opened her eyes. She couldn't believe how clear it was.

The bubbling stream flowed out of the ground near the caves and pooled in a bowl of rocks and coral pieces. There were a few fish that swam by her as she explored underwater. She came up for air. "This is amazing."

For Ryleigh, moments like this were as good as sunken chests of gold and jewels. This was the living treasure, the miracle of art created by sea and sun.

She splashed around and washed away the dirt and grime from the last few days of working on the island. Her hair was a tangled, chestnut mess underwater as she frolicked in the clean, clear water.

At one point, she swam around the lagoon finding areas that were shallow enough for her to stand with her head and shoulders out of the water. She finished her bath and then swam to the edge of the pool of water. She got out and stood at the side where the hill ended and the stream rolled out into the sea. The view from the promontory allowed her to scan the sea in three directions.

"Why didn't Elliot bring me here?"

In the beautiful sunlight, she could see the gale winds coming in from the southeast, pushing the turbulent ocean into giant cresting waves that cascaded into foaming whitecaps. She sat down on a rock and dried her hands with her bandana. She reached for the folded paper again.

She studied it from the stream and this location's offered point of view.

Then she saw it. Her gaze at the white caps that dotted the sea matched up similarly with the small dots on the map. "These aren't bushes. It's water?"

The water from the stream pooled near the caves to create an occasional horsetail-looking waterfall.

The caves. The caves behind the small waterfall. "What's in the caves? And how do I swim underwater long enough to get into the cave opening without drowning?"

Something she would plan to do tomorrow or the day after tomorrow. Knowing Ebba could feed herself still gave Ryleigh little comfort, in that she wasn't there in time to give the cat food and water; and it was getting late, so she wanted to journey back to camp. She was excited about her day's adventures and knew she would need to plan every detail of the cave exploration. She only had four more days until Elliot returned, and she wanted to make sure she was there waiting when he flew back to rescue her.

TWELVE

CHICAGO

ELLIOT FINN STEPPED onto the landing strip and was greeted by a black ragtop jeep. He jumped into the front seat.

"Hello, Dice." Elliot was glad to see his boss.

"Hi, Elliot. How's Director Pierce?" His boss was wearing a dark navy suit with a light chambray blue shirt and a red tie.

"Useless. Like we thought." Elliot took off his jacket and then pulled his t-shirt over his head. "They couldn't agree to delay for a few days." Since the President was unavailable, he had met with the Director.

"So the testing will continue?"

"Yes. They talked about how it was the perfect area, geographically speaking." Elliot unzipped his pants and tossed them with the rest of the pile of clothes into the backseat.

"Well, it is better than what we've seen in the state of Oklahoma. It's astounding how these manmade earthquakes are tied to gas and oil exploration."

"They have more quakes than California?"

"God yes. Prior to 2009, there were on average two earthquakes a year in Oklahoma, that were a magnitude of three of greater. Last year, there were nine hundred and seventy." Dice sped the jeep through the first yellow stop light, but slammed on the brakes at the next red light.

"970?"

"That's right. 970. The vast majority are small, causing little damage."

"But what I fear is that what these little tremors around the islands lack in punch, they'll make up in volume." Elliot retrieved a gray duffle bag from the backseat. He unzipped it and pulled out a white button-down shirt. He talked to Dice while buttoning the shirt. "Did you get the files and photos?"

"Yes, got them. And your family they're safe and sound. I saw them myself. You'll have plenty of time to clean up and get dressed before the trial. She's on the docket for 3:00 this afternoon. We have four hours."

"Yeah, about the trial."

"What? You can't back out now!" Dice swerved the car when he looked at Elliot and yelled.

"The hell, I can't. And watch the road." Elliot slipped his pants on and zipped the fly while half standing up in the convertible jeep.

"But we're counting on you to be there."

"I got you the girl and the testimony, that's all you need."

"What if Dexco doesn't buy it?"

"They will. It's the judge and attorneys, I'd be worried about if I were you. How's her tan look?"

"Very brown, but doesn't look fake."

"That's good."

They sat in silence for a few minutes while Elliot continued to primp his hair and tie a black tie around his neck while looking in the visor mirror.

He pulled out a revolver from the duffle bag and pulled up a suit pant leg, and cuffed on a small ankle holster.

"You can't bring your piece into the courtroom," Dice said, watching Elliot.

"I said, I'm not going."

"Elliot, come on, don't be a dick about this. You have to at least stay for her testimony, which will start promptly at 3."

"I can't, Dice. I have too much to do before flying out." Truth was, he didn't want to see her. It would be too hard to look into those questioning emerald eyes. He'd be afraid she would see what he felt, and then the whole plan could be messed up, if she knew the truth.

Dice pulled off the main road and turned the jeep down a small gravel road. Then he pulled the jeep into Lover's Diner. *Figures*, Elliot thought to himself.

"Are you ready?" Dice asked.

"Ready."

Elliot's thoughts went to Dexco's CEO and how he had to get to him, to let the slimy toad know he couldn't go around kidnapping his family.

THIRTEEN

THEY BOTH got out of the state-issued rental vehicle and Elliot opened the door of the diner. Before the door could shut, Elliot heard, "Uncle El." And he felt two sets of small little arms wrap around his waist. He picked up his youngest niece and hugged her tight.

"How's my sweet niece, Emily?"

"Super-duper. Did you know we were on a vacation?" Emily asked.

This brought a burn to Elliot's eyes as he tried to look away and avoid her sweet smile. He set her down and stood up to face his brother, Ron.

Ron and Elliot embraced and gave each other strong smacks on the back.

"You're too thin, Elliot," Ron said with a knowing look in his eyes.

"God, it's great to see you three. I don't know what I would have done if anything happened to you." Elliot looked around the café and noticed it was filled with plain clothes bodyguards and FBI personnel. "You brought the cavalry and then some."

"No, they're compliments of the FBI or DIA, or FDA; I'm not sure who's on whose side anymore. Jesus, brother, what are you mixed up in?"

"It's a long story– "

"–and you can't share it with me yet."

"That's right. I'm sorry, bro." Elliot smacked his hand across his shoulder. "Are they treating you okay now?"

"Like the king and queen, and their two princesses."

"How's Patty taking all of this? Is she holding out?" Elliot still stood at the end of the counter of the diner. His two nieces had returned to the red leather booth and had their faces buried into an old fashioned glass filled with chocolate ice cream, and lots of whip cream and cherries.

"Why don't you come to dinner tonight, and ask her yourself. We'd love to have you with us, and that would help get us back to normalcy."

"I can't."

"Of course you can't," Ron said with disappointment and sarcasm ringing from his voice.

"Not tonight. But soon." Elliot seemed distracted as he looked around the café. He still wanted to know who was the leak on the team. He knew that the main reason his brother and two nieces were here, alive and well this afternoon, was because the team had let it leak out that Ryleigh Lane was dead and long gone, and wouldn't be able to testify in the trial this afternoon. Part of the plan. His brother and nieces had been held hostage in a confined environment with little communication. To the outside world and his family, it had looked like they'd been on a paid vacation that Ron won in his company's sweepstakes. Secretly, it had all been planned and arranged to threaten Elliot into doing what he was told.

Now that everyone in his family was safe, it was time for the team to move in. Time to make the arrest. Today, after the testimony of the star witness.

FOURTEEN

CHANDLER PULLED up to a stop sign, and a homeless man jumped out into the street and sprayed his windshield with cleaner.

"Come on. Get the hell away from my car!" he yelled out the window. "Oh man, look at the mess you're making. This is a rental car. I don't care how clean it is." Chandler laid on the horn, and the man backed off and retreated to the curb.

His thoughts were on the exotic island he was traveling to later that evening. It had been quite a challenge to get there. Turns out there's no tourism on Keg Key, and it could only be visited by smaller ships because of the coral reefs surrounding the atolls. He picked up his cell, hit speaker, and dialed a number.

"Did you come up with anything?"

"It depends on what you mean by anything."

"The car."

"Yeah, the address where it's registered is in Naperville."

"Okay. Thought so." Chandler was on his way to the Dexco CEO's home in the suburbs of Naperville.

"It's registered to his old lady."

"His wife?"

"Yeah. Christine Edersom."

Chandler found that a bit odd, but who knew, maybe it had to do with avoiding taxes. "Maybe a gift to her. What about the scientist?"

"Whoever tipped him off about you looking into it has gone to great lengths to hide this guy."

"How do you know?"

"The server with all his data has been wiped clean. It doesn't look like identity theft."

Chandler pulled down a street in a low income neighborhood. In the area he was entering, most of the houses and apartments looked condemned and in various stages of being knocked down. Many lots were vacant. The debris from the houses that had been knocked down had piled up and become overgrown with trees and weeds.

"Detective, what do you think?" The voice on the other side of the phone paused. "Chandler, are you there?"

"Let me call you back." He clicked off the phone, sliding it into his shirt pocket while verifying the address on the notepad. He was in the right place.

"Hmm. Why would a guy that registers his two hundred-thousand-dollar car in his wife's name want to live in a neighborhood like this?" He figured his wife dressed in St. Laurent and designer duds, dined at the latest posh restaurants, and was of a privileged breed of women whose high-end lifestyle was due to her marriage to a rich and famous husband.

The street he'd turned onto was miserable, poorly paved, and trailing toward a bad neighborhood. He drove forward cautiously, watching the surroundings. He arrived in front of the house listed on his paper.

He parked at the curb. No signs of anyone on the street, or in the house. No lights on. He searched the front porch as he approached and pounded on the wood frame door. Waited. No answer.

He walked down the driveway to the back of the house, peering into the garage window. No cars.

"Definitely not a red Ferrari inside."

Suddenly, a strong hand slammed against the back of his neck, grasping him into a head lock. He smelt perspiration.

Chandler wasn't usually scared, but he struggled to get free and didn't succeed. He was jerked back and then a terrifying hit exploded onto his chin. His knees became numb, and Chandler was out cold.

FIFTEEN

FIFTH DISTRICT COURT

THE COURTROOM, once church silent, awakened as everyone stood up with the entrance of U.S. District Judge Baker. He moved with confident, long strides, his shiny black shoes peeking out from under his robe with each step.

A few rows behind Greg Edersom, a cell phone jingled a familiar tune, but Greg couldn't place the song. His mind was filled with loathing and boredom. The jingle continued one more time before it went silent. *That should piss off the judge,* he thought.

A startled bailiff cleared his throat, and said, "As a reminder, all mobile devices should be checked at the desk." He stared at the middle of the row behind Greg.

"Excuse me. I'm sorry, your honor." There was a rustling of papers and then a shuffling of feet as a young, fairly hot reporter moved out of the row, everyone scooting aside to let her by.

The courtroom door creaked open and slammed closed as she left. The judge sat down, clearly perturbed. "Does anyone else care to leave? Or can we continue with the trial?" It appeared that the one ringing phone had tested his patience beyond irritation.

Greg wrapped his long, sweaty fingers around his water glass, sitting on the defendant table. He watched the jurors' reactions to the judge, and felt he could read most of their minds. He had, in the last ten days, managed in his mind to name them all, and to assign occupations or jobs to each and every juror (and even given some families). He felt he knew them better than the lawyers, even his own one-thousand-and-fifty dollar an hour lawyer.

Even before he'd been named as CEO of Dexco Pharmaceuticals, he'd had an uncanny knack for guessing what strangers did for a living, based on very few indicators. He made a game of it.

With over thirty thousand employees world-wide, he still liked to be involved in the hiring process, often asking his secretary to not tell him what job an applicant was applying for. The job applicants could range from a warehouse pill assembly line supervisor, to janitor, to software analyst, to vice president of marketing, and without so much as even a name or a resume in front of him, he could, most times, accurately guess what job they were pursuing. He could guess the salary they made within two thousand dollars. Sure, there were a few applicants that fooled him. But more often than not, he was successful at his game.

One of the few he had misjudged had been Ryleigh Lane. A bright, gorgeous, thirty-something-year-old girl who now preoccupied his conscience during most of the trial.

From the day he had met her, Greg Edersom hadn't been able to figure out the job Ryleigh Lane was applying for, and he couldn't pin her down, nor her motivations. This one employee, he had misjudged. He had been way off.

He ran his eyes across the jurors' faces again, checking out their attitudes after the lunch break. Mr. Joe Bob looked like he'd eaten at the bar-b-q shack again, and he had bitty chunks of rib pieces stuck in his teeth. And Joe Bob was wishing he had thought to grab a toothpick. Julie and Martha had eaten at the deli. *They're beginning to be friends*, he thought. The middle-aged man, Jacob, in the front row, was already dying to smoke a cigarette.

His thoughts wandered back to her. *Poor Ryleigh.* Unfortunately, the ex-Dexco Director of Quality Control would not be able to be called as a witness in the class action suit against his company. He knew she would have been trouble. She had been three years and six months into the job that she'd seemed to work eighteen hours a day at, mainly late into the night, when she'd come across falsified documents.

Or so she said. But he wasn't buying it.

These were documents that could potentially destroy and withdraw Dexco's new, hot diabetes drug.

Currently, Ms. Ryleigh Lane was stranded and more likely dead in the middle of the sea, God-knew-where. No chance to hear from that star witness.

"The court will resume. Mr. Smith, your turn to call your next witness," the judge said to the plaintiff's chief lawyer.

"If it pleases the court, we wish to call Ryleigh Lane," Mr. Smith said.

Greg squirmed in the chair and whispered in his lawyer's ear, "I thought they couldn't locate her."

"Me, too. But maybe they did," his lawyer whispered back.

The court door creaked open, and the room filled with the minute rustle of the jurors, the spectators, and the lawyers all craning their necks at the next witness.

Greg knew it was only a messenger there to indeed tell the lawyer that Ryleigh Lane could not be located. He knew Elliot Finn had had a hand in helping with the messy job of losing Ryleigh. The girl was either dead or alone on an island, stranded. And if she was truly still stranded, the scientists' quakes would take care of her.

Greg focused on Joe Bob's face. He'd appeared to lose interest in picking his teeth. His eyes had lit up like he'd just seen a gorgeous woman enter the courtroom.

Greg couldn't handle the anticipation. He turned his head sideways, at about the time a woman in a navy straight skirt with tan legs passed by, her slim backside toward him.

Why wasn't she stopping at the lawyer's table?

"Hello, Ms. Lane," the bailiff said as he directed her to the witness chair.

Greg Edersom, for the first time in his life, felt the blood drain from his face as he stared at Ryleigh Lane being sworn in. And before she solemnly swore to tell the truth, the whole truth, and nothing but the truth, she grinned over at Greg.

PART 2

CALEIGH

*X marks the spot, with a dot, dot, dot and a
dash, dash, dash, and a big question mark!
The water trickles up, the water trickles
down, and the water trickles all around.
Crack!*

Author Unknown

SIXTEEN

CALEIGH

OKAY, SO SHE WAS lying, before God and the whole courtroom.

She wasn't Ryleigh Lane.

She was Caleigh Lane, Ryleigh's monozygotic twin.

Caleigh was careful not to actually push her hand firmly onto the Bible, or anything around her, because contrary to what most people think, identical twins have the same DNA, but not the same fingerprints.

Ryleigh and she were indistinguishable in every way. They looked alike, sounded alike, and thought alike. Several times in the last few days, Caleigh had picked up the phone at Ryleigh's condo and carried on a fifteen minute conversation with Elliot, and he'd said it was like talking to Ryleigh. Caleigh was preparing for the trial. She was careful to avoid all the calls from Ryleigh's Dexco colleagues. They had no idea that she, Caleigh Lane, even existed. And still didn't. By the look on Greg Edersom's face, he felt like he'd seen a ghost. Ryleigh Lane back from the island. *Surprise! She wasn't dead.*

Caleigh would have sworn on a stack of Spiderman comic books if giving her oath helped Ryleigh. Oh, you bet your sweet ass, she'd tell the truth and the whole truth, so help her God. Even if telling the truth meant a perjured testimony. In this case, the only lie being told was who was delivering the truth. But Caleigh was not perjuring herself; she was planning to be truthful under oath, having just lied about who was delivering the truth.

"You may have a seat, Ms. Lane."

"Ryleigh." Caleigh sat down and grinned slightly over at the jurors. "Call me Ryleigh."

She thought that if any of the bad guys entered the courtroom who had any idea about her twin being stranded, then her cover would be blown. But she wasn't worried about that. There was no reason for anyone to think Ryleigh was stranded and not able to attend court. Except for the bad guys.

There'd been a few stories about the cruise ship – the accident – in the newspapers, but there hadn't been any mention of missing people, only survivors and those killed. So, where did that leave the case? Was anyone looking for her sister? She had been told by Elliot that a detective had interviewed Ryleigh's neighbors. She knew his name was Chandler. Caleigh found herself happy that Detective Chandler could be out looking for missing passengers, like Ryleigh. Even knowing that Elliot would be there to rescue her soon.

Caleigh had recently returned to Chicago after sixteen years. After Elliot had found her in Italy. After he'd told her about her sister's predicament.

"Caleigh, you have to come back to the States. You can do this for her. I know she would do the same thing for you," he had pleaded with her.

Of course, she'd agreed. She loved her sister and would do anything to save her. Caleigh wanted to help Ryleigh and to avenge Greg. That was what really thrilled her, taking down Dexco Pharmaceuticals and him with it.

She had stopped by Ryleigh's condo to get Ry's clothes, shoes, and handbag for the trial, and a neighbor may have spotted her. She had spent a few days there, holed up and preparing for the trial. Surely, someone could have seen her and thought she was Ryleigh.

It wouldn't be the first time Caleigh had pretended to be her twin sister. They had swapped identities when they were in middle school, but only for a weekend. No one had ever figured it out, not even their parents.

When they had grown up together on Central Ave in the yellow house, they had been inseperable. But once they had made it to high school, like everyone else, they had their ups and downs. They had crazy teenage emotions and raging hormones to deal with, but they made it through together. Then their parents had been tragically killed in a car accident, and they hadn't been able to handle the pain, so they'd gone their separate ways. Caleigh had left to live with their grandparents and to study in Italy while Ryleigh had stayed in the U.S. Her sister had become a loner and eventually graduated, and taken the job at Dexco, working long hours. Ryleigh wouldn't let anyone into her life. She feared getting hurt by another loss. That included Caleigh. Ryleigh had never told anyone at Dexco she had a sister, let alone an identical twin sister.

Now Caleigh was pretending to be her. Caleigh had needed to learn a lot relatively fast. Which was easy to do, since she had one strong trait that her duplicate sister didn't have – a photographic memory. She could memorize vast amounts of material without effort. But her crash course of Ryleigh's job data that Elliot had provided her was no substitute for actually having done the work or understanding the daily Dexco details. The cross-examination could be a bitch. Even though Caleigh could recall details from her memory, she might not remember the meaning. The good news was that Ryleigh wasn't a scientist, so she wouldn't necessarily understand what she had read – only that these missing documents existed.

As Caleigh thought about this now, she felt a knot in her stomach, and she tried to appear calm – which came across as the opposite.

"Are you okay, Ms. Lane?" the tall plaintiff asked.

"Yes. Sorry, just a bit nervous," she said, and shot a glance at the jurors for sympathy. That was the truth. She was nervous. A few jurors looked in her eyes. Good. *This is for you, Ryleigh.*

"Are you ready?" Her lawyer asked – actually, Ryleigh's prudish lawyer asked.

"Yes," she answered.

For a second, she thought that Greg was going to launch his body across the defendant's table and strangle her. But instead the horrid CEO leaned over and whispered in his lawyer's ear, and before they could get started with the questions, the defendant's lawyer stood up.

"Judge, if you may, we'd like a recess. We were told this witness was not available for testimony. I need a little time to confer with my colleagues," Dexco's lawyer said.

Caleigh sat there staring at Greg. He avoided her eyes by looking around the courtroom, and then back at her, frowning.

"Jurors, it's your lucky day. We will resume tomorrow morning at 9 AM. Ms. Lane, thank you for your time," the judge said. "We will hear your testimony tomorrow."

Caleigh looked at Greg. He smiled a little. She stepped down from the witness stand and stopped to consult with her lawyer. While she stood there, she could feel Greg Edersom's eyes burning into her back. Her legs shook in relief from avoiding the testimony and from the hatred-filled eyes burning into her.

SEVENTEEN

CALEIGH STEPPED OUTSIDE the courthouse, aware that she didn't have to hide her eyes under sunglasses anymore, like she had the last few days. The air was crisp and cool for October, as if nature was preparing an entrance for a cold autumn. People were flocking along the lakefront, tourists and locals bustling to happy hours or home from work.

Her little Italian town didn't have rush-hour. She just loved all the electricity in the air. It was invigorating.

Poor Ryleigh had nothing at all. Her heart sank when she thought of her. She often thought of her twin. Like last month, she had felt sharp pains in her wrist. She remembered rubbing her right wrist one morning and not knowing why. When she had met Elliot, he'd told her about Ryleigh's snake bite – on her right wrist. Caleigh didn't believe in all the stories of twins feeling each other's joy and sorrow, but today in the courtroom, she'd imagined Ryleigh feeling a small triumph in her gut. That everything was going as planned. And knowing that in her heart Elliot would be there in a few days to bring her home.

Caleigh sat on the bench where she had first met Elliot. Chicagoans were soaking in the sun as the autumn came to a close. Soon the skies would turn gray and the lake would freeze over as the icy blasts of winter descended on their city.

The sky grew dark, prompting her to relinquish her park bench. She wanted to grab a taxi back to the condo and prepare for the next day on the witness stand.

Caleigh was about a foot from the curb when, from out of nowhere, a black car sped up behind her, threw open the door, and the driver said, "Get in." He didn't need to ask her twice. She jumped in the passenger side and the car lurched off with a screech.

EIGHTEEN
KEG KEY

I'M OBSESSED. I'm crazy to want to wake up each day and follow a treasure map around a deserted island. But it has its benefits. It's kept my mind off my predicament.

"If the map is for real, and I find something, I could be a hero when I'm rescued," Ryleigh said to Ebba, the white furball rolling in the sand while she fished off the rocks.

She didn't feel like a hero, and no amount of gold or jewels would change that. Some might say she was a hero because she had saved lives by staying out of sight that day Elliot had been rescued. Just five days earlier. She had saved her life and his life, not to mention his brother, Ron, and his family.

She had a small laugh. Her great act of heroism, the most important thing she had ever done, and she couldn't talk to a soul about it.

Ryleigh had saved another life, too; Ashley, or Ash, her friend. Ashley was an acquaintance from Chicago, in the drug trial group. Ryleigh had been a hero to her, too.

She focused her watery eyes on the cat. "I won't be able to stand it here for much longer." She was lonely and, if Elliot didn't return for her soon, she would fade away, becoming a small fraction of the person she'd once been.

How had Elliot been so tangled up with the bad folks? How had she fallen in love with someone who'd lied to get her onto this island? And how could she believe he would come back for her? She had gotten so used to the lies and the deceit, that maybe his plan to return for her was a lie, too.

Maybe, it had occurred to her, he wouldn't return in ten days. Her head was pounding. Ten days. Would she be able to make it through ten days of this lonely life? Even if Elliot rescued her, would she go back to Chicago?

The next five days would be crucial, but Ryleigh was determined to change the rules. The next five days *could* be the game-changer.

She wouldn't let someone else be a hero. Not this time.

To clear her brain, Ryleigh began to sing a song that she'd known as a child. One that seemed more apt for her life this last month.

"Smile, though my heart is aching, smile, even though it's breaking, when there's clouds in the sky, I'll get by. If I smile through my sorrow, smile, and maybe tomorrow, I'll see the sun come shining through for me... as time goes by...." She couldn't remember all the verses. She sang the same lines over and over as she sat fishing on the rocks. When she finished, she had tears pricking her eyes and, before she knew it, tears falling down her cheeks.

NINETEEN

SHE CRIED A LOT these days. Back home, Ryleigh had hardly ever cried over the years. She'd cried a lifetime of tears when she'd been a teenager. Caleigh and Ryleigh had cried a lot when they'd lost their parents. They would hug each other and cry in a huddle. She'd thought her heart would never heal.

The pain in her heart now was similar to that pain she'd had that year as a teenage girl. She had lost Caleigh after their parent's accident. She had grown tough. Now Elliot had taken a piece of her heart.

No matter how much pain she was in, there had to be something inside of her that was stronger than the pain.

She felt her throat hurt as a lump formed and tears welled in her eyes. Something inside of her had kept her surviving here, and it had kept her surviving back then, after the accident. Like a survivor that wants to live to tell their story. It was stubbornness. It was this inner something that had allowed her to go on in the face of tremendous loss.

Ryleigh recalled all the vivid, surrealistic details of that evening. The evening of their parents' accident. The gooey cheese pizza Caleigh and she had made while Mom and Dad were out on *date night*. The smell of popcorn lingering in the air as they giggled at the latest *Friends* episode. She remembered Chandler and Monica had been dating in that show. The two had slept together at Ross's wedding the season before. The twins had loved watching *Friends* every week, and their parents had given them that night together. But it wasn't a sacrifice for them. Their parents had loved their *date night* together, too.

She remembered the doorbell ringing, and the glances Caleigh and she had made at each other. *Who could that be?* They peeked out the window, and she felt a chill run down her back. There was a Cook County sheriff's car parked in their driveway, and two policeman on their porch.

Caleigh cautiously opened the door.

"Are you the daughters of Joan and Thomas Lane?" the taller of the two policemen asked.

"Yes," Ryleigh replied in a whisper, instinctively grabbing Caleigh's hand.

"Can we come in?" he asked.

"Our parents aren't here. They're at the movies," Caleigh said.

"Please, it's okay to let us in." One policeman took out his badge and showed it to them.

"Okay," she said, holding the door open.

From there, it was all like a dream. Like a bad nightmare. He asked if they had a nearby relative they could call. They asked why.

"We have our aunt that lives in Michigan. What's wrong? What's happened?" Caleigh asked.

"What about grandparents?" he asked without answering Caleigh.

"Our mom's parents live in Italy," Ryleigh replied. "Dad's parents aren't alive." Her stomach was doing flip-flops and she felt the cheesy pizza forcing its way out.

"The roads were icy," he'd said. And she remembered Caleigh crying in her ears. Screaming. Or was that her own screaming? She remembered that the policeman in the tight shirt had kept talking and Caleigh and her had been crying and sobbing. "The truck swerved into their lane and your dad's car hit the curb, and the icy curve that had caused it to flip..." he said.

She wanted to hit him, to tell him to shut up, and to get out of their house. And to just wait until their parents got home. He had it all wrong.

"They're gone. I'm so sorry for your loss."

Then people kept coming to their house, bringing food, making "arrangements", crying, and asking her and Caleigh if they were okay. "Fucking no, we're not okay. Our parents are dead. They left us all alone. How could we ever be okay? Ever again?"

Ryleigh remembered she'd been just sort of blank during the whole funeral process, and had wanted it to be over. Everyone had been crying. All she remembered was snow and tears.

The surviving twins had formed a plan that took them on separate journeys. Caleigh left for Italy to live with their grandparents immediately after the funeral. Ryleigh stayed with her aunt in Michigan, and moved back to Chicago the day after she graduated from high school. Their sweet, yellow house on Central Street had been sold. She'd used the money she got when she turned eighteen to go to college. And she'd never looked back.

Caleigh, she had heard, was a goat farmer and made cheese. Which made her laugh. If only Caleigh could see her. "I'm living on an island, Caleigh, catching my own fish, and surviving."

Ryleigh thought she would go to Italy after Elliot rescued her. She was ready to face the past. Caleigh was family, and the only person she could trust. They'd had a wary truce put in place the day they'd turned twenty-one, when they'd learned more about their family's history and secrets.

Grumpy, exhausted, frustrated, silent tears welled up again and slid down her cheeks, and she brushed them aside. She looked out at the beautiful, deep blue sea and mouthed silently, "God, I'd really like a do-over of this year."

"When I get back to the States, I'm just going to disappear into the seething mass of humanity in Chicago, or maybe I won't go back there. Maybe Italy."

She finished catching and cleaning the fish and fried it with oil on the open fire pit. She heard a shuffling noise in the brush near the tiki hut. *The feral hog?* Maybe she should make a fence around the tiki hut.

After breakfast, she carried the last of the lawn chairs to the campground and positioned them around the hut. Without her Hunk-a-berry Finn, she would have to learn to fend for herself.

She looked at her cat with two different colored eyes perched at her ankles. Ryleigh was the last of the Ahoy Cruise passengers. There had used to be two. Now there was just one left. The city one.

TWENTY

ELLIOT FLASHED A quick smile at Caleigh before he drove the rental car away from the curb. He had been in Chicago for one hour and had debated about whether he should show up at the courthouse until he had received a call that the trial was finished for the day. He'd had a hunch he'd find Caleigh here in the park where they'd once met.

"Hi, Elliot, good to see you. I thought you would be in the courtroom today," she said.

"Hello, Caleigh." He nodded, his lips pressed together. He reached over and hugged her with his free arm. She leaned in and half-hugged him in return. He could feel the chill of her hand, and smell the faintest trace of perfume. He thought of Ryleigh, and how she would never feel cold air on the island, and how she never got to wear perfume.

"I'm starved. Can we grab a bite to eat?"

"That's the plan," Elliot said. "I know just the spot."

Elliot sat in his usual corner table, his back to the wall, eyes on the door. The restaurant was close to the safe house and the staff treated him like royalty, and they were discreet. The restaurant was dim, the tables candle-lit with a few shaded bulbs on the walls, and the carpets were a deep shade of blue. All around them, the walls were decorated with wooden-framed pictures of celebrities and dignitaries. If anyone came to the restaurant and asked the staff who they had seen, they would say, "I can't recall."

They ate an early dinner together. Elliot wasn't hungry, but he forced himself to eat. He picked at his food. Caleigh worked hard to clean her plate. She was dressed in a navy jacket with gold buttons, this draped over a white starched blouse and a pencil-slim skirt. She wore navy pumps with a gold buckle. No hose. Dice had been right, her legs were tan.

"Any news about the island?" Caleigh asked.

"You know I can't discuss it," he replied. He ached when he looked into Caleigh's eyes. He had thought Ryleigh was the most beautiful women he had ever met, and there across the table from him was her identical duplicate. Caleigh's emerald green eyes with flecks of gold, heavily lashed, piercing, all-knowing, were the same as Ryleigh's eyes.

Caleigh shook her head. "Are you okay?"

"I'm–" he couldn't finish. He stared at his half-eaten plate of pasta.

"–I know. I think about her, too. Every second I'm on that stand tomorrow, it's for her. It's funny, I hadn't worried about Ryleigh while I was away in Italy. I knew she'd be okay. But the last few months, it's felt different."

She sliced off a piece of steak, and pushed it around her plate.

"Not hungry?"

"I can't eat much. I'm upset over Ryleigh. Worried about her welfare."

"I worry, too. She should be fine for a few more days. Are you ready for tomorrow?" He knew she was well-prepared, but he wanted to change the subject. Away from Ryleigh.

"Ready as can be. Did you bring the notebook?"

"Yes, I left it in the safe house." Elliot had made plans to hide Caleigh away from Ryleigh's apartment, once Greg found out this afternoon that she was back from the island. He hadn't wanted to risk the Dexco thugs coming by to snatch her before the trial.

He watched her as she stared at her food. It could have been Ryleigh sitting across the table from him and he wouldn't have known the difference. They were mirror images of each other. Maybe Caleigh's eyes were set a little farther apart, but he knew that most likely they were not.

The door opened and Elliot met eyes with a young girl in her late twenties. She smiled at him and then turned to look at Caleigh. Her expression changed immediately.

The girl approached their table the way someone might encounter a celebrity – tentative, her eyes full of excitement and interest. She was wearing a black, mid-calf dress, and her blonde hair was cut short in a boyish style.

It wasn't Elliot she was looking at. She'd recognized Caleigh.

Staring at Caleigh through squinted eyes, as the girl became accustomed to the dark restaurant, in a loud, concerned voice, she almost yelled, "Ryleigh!"

Caleigh physically jumped and shot a glance at Elliot. He nodded at Caleigh and shrugged.

Caleigh turned to the girl, looking up at her, not recognizing her. She smiled and said, "Hi."

The girl grabbed her and they hugged. "What..." the girl said, "what are you doing here?"

"Laundry?" Caleigh smiled. "I'm doing laundry."

The girl flipped her head back and laughed a way-to-loud laugh. Then she quickly looked over at Elliot. "Is this him? Is this your secret lover?"

Elliot didn't blush, but he realized that this girl must have known Ryleigh intimately in order to know she'd had an out-of-town boyfriend.

"Hi, I'm Elliot." He held his hand out to her.

"Woo, wee. You're a doll. "She shook his hand and looked from Elliot to Caleigh, and winked. "I can see you're from Florida. You're so tan."

It was true. Elliot's skin was still abnormally tanned a dark glow after his month on the island with Ryleigh. Caleigh smiled, but hadn't uttered another word since her joke about the laundry.

The girl stepped back. "Ryleigh, what happened to you? Last we spoke, you were going on a cruise? Then I never heard back from you."

"We did," Caleigh finally replied.

Elliot jumped in. "That's why we're so tan. And you are?"

She flipped her head and her hair bounced on her shoulders. "How rude of me. I'm Ashley Nelson. You can call me Ash."

"How do you two know each other?" Elliot asked.

"Ryleigh saved my life." The girl grinned, and reached around and hugged Caleigh again.

TWENTY-ONE

HER HEART stopped racing. Thank goodness Elliot could jump in and run interference. Of course, Caleigh had no idea who Ashley – Ash – was. She searched her memory for an Ashley Nelson amongst all the Dexco employees, and couldn't find one. Seeing one of her twin sister's friends had startled her, though she'd anticipated seeing people at the trial and had memorized all the faces with the names.

She knew Ashley was waiting for her to reply with a Ryleigh explanation of how she'd saved this girl's life. Caleigh had to guess she had meant Ryleigh saved her life figuratively.

"Well, I saved your life, figuratively speaking," Caleigh said, trying to act completely like Ryleigh's character.

Ashley looked at her with her lips drawn tight, her black boots clicking together. For a moment, Caleigh thought she might try to prove Caleigh was lying about who she was. But that would be ridicules. This girl really thinks she's talking to Caleigh's twin sister, Ryleigh.

"You didn't tell Elliot?" Ashley said to her, sounding disappointed.

"Some of it," she said, looking to Elliot for help.

He looked at his watch. "We have to go, Ryleigh. I'd love to hear the details someday. We should all have a drink next week."

Ashley nodded. "I should be the one buying you dinner. Can I tell him?" she asked Caleigh.

"Sure," she shrugged, having no idea what Ashely was going to tell about her sister. "We have a few minutes."

Elliot raised his hand at the waiter and motioned for the check. He also typed a text on his phone.

"Well, your girlfriend here works for the company... "Ashley stopped and looked at her. "I forget their name."

"Dexco," she said. "Dexco Pharmaceuticals." So that ruled out that Ryleigh and Ashley worked together.

"Yes, that's it." She smiled and padded Caleigh on the shoulder. A gesture she found odd.

Ashley watched as a waiter gave the check to Elliot, but she kept talking. "Ryleigh knew about the drug in the study," she said, again touching Caleigh's shoulder.

Both she and Elliot looked up at her more carefully. How did she know about the drug? How close were Ryleigh and Ashley?

Caleigh knew Ashley was waiting for her to say something, but Elliot jumped in. "The diabetes trial for their new miracle drug."

"Yes!" Ashley looked surprised. "I thought you hadn't told him." Her eyes were accusing her of getting caught in a lie.

"Well, he knows a lot more than you think, "she said. "We've been alone for a while on the cruise."

"Oh, of course," Ashley almost apologized.

"So, go on. Tell me how my sweet Ryleigh here saved your life," Elliot urged her.

The whole conversation was frustrating, but necessary. This was a great test for Caleigh for tomorrow's trial. She smiled and nodded at Ashley. "It's okay, Ash."

"Well, Ryleigh approached me and asked if we could meet for coffee. She said she wanted to discuss the drug we were taking in the study," Ashley said.

Caleigh was more confused. How had Ryleigh known the people in the study group? Had she actually reached out to them?

Ashley lowered her head close in to her and Elliot, and whispered, "That's when she told me that the new diabetes drug we took had issues, and urged me to get out of the trial group."

Caleigh wondered why her sister would have been telling a stranger this. "Yes, I did," she replied.

"At first I didn't believe her. But when she stopped going to the meetings and got out of the trial herself, well, I believed her then." Ashley squeezed her hand.

Caleigh wondered what she'd meant about Ryleigh getting out of the trial herself.

"And then we heard about two people in our group that got sick, heart attacks or something, and died! Oh, I know it was all a coincidence and Dexco people kept urging us to stay in the trial."

"Thank God we talked about it."

"I know and I'm out. I don't care. I've had minor changes in the dose of my Lantus insulin, and I take my short-acting insulin shots three times a day now." She straightened her dress and turned toward the door.

The waiter brought the check, handing it to Elliot.

"I'll leave you two alone. Great meeting you, Elliot, and seeing you, Ryleigh."

"Let's catch up later," Caleigh said.

"Sure, let's do."

Caleigh still found it hard to believe Ryleigh would just confide in a stranger in a study. She reached for the paper napkin under her water glass and started twisting it. "It was great seeing you, too, Ashley. Take care, and good luck with your meds." She didn't know what else to say.

"You, too." A frown formed on Ashley's face. "Sorry, I forgot to ask you. Is the honeymoon phase of your diabetes over? I mean, has your pancreas stopped secreting insulin totally now? I thought it might take a few months." She looked at Elliot, "It did for me. A few months and then it stopped. I just increased my insulin injections."

Caleigh froze in the chair. A chill ran down her back. Ryleigh and diabetes? *No, that can't be true. Ryleigh is sick? Poor Ry. Aren't we identical? Wouldn't I have signs, too? Wouldn't Elliot have known?*

Worry sparked like two naked wires crossed.

"Are you okay, Ryleigh? You look like you've seen a ghost." She pulled out her cell phone. "Let's get a selfie."

"What?" Caleigh asked.

Before she could react, Ashley leaned over toward Caleigh and extended her arm out, and snapped a photo.

"No, that's not a good idea," Elliot protested, but it was too late.

They all said their goodbyes and Ashley went toward the bar.

"Come on. I need to get you out of here. She's probably posted that photo all over social media, and the wrong people may be looking for you." Elliot signed the check and stood up.

Caleigh was still shocked over the news about Ryleigh. She tried to remain calm, and told Elliot she had to use the restroom before they left.

She prayed she'd make it to the ladies' bathroom before losing her dinner.

TWENTY-TWO

CALEIGH RUSHED to the bathroom. The stalls were empty. She positioned her head over the toilet, feeling like she would throw up. While fighting the nausea, she heard the bathroom door open and, half squatting on the floor, she noticed the large brown tasseled loafers outside the stall in front of her, which didn't belong to a female.

She frantically reached for her phone and silently texted Elliot. As soon as she hit *send*, she felt the metal stall door kicked open. Her sense of a pending threat had been accurate, and she prayed Elliot would receive her text sooner than later.

She was shoved violently forward. Still kneeling on the floor, she couldn't see her assailant. His gloved hand grabbed her around the neck, one of the tasseled shoes kicked the toilet seat up, and before Caleigh could gurgle a scream, he shoved her head in the cold toilet water. She struggled for air. The man squeezed harder around her neck, and she felt water filling her eyes, nose, ears, and lungs. She had a terrible fear she was going to drown in the porcelain bowl, but right before her lungs burst from a burning pain, his grip released.

In a throaty voice, he said, "You better be careful on what information you say tomorrow on the stand."

She gasped and gagged and tried to reply, but only squeaky sounds came out. She turned and saw the face of the loafer-shoed man. He was a short, stocky man with a red, bloated face with a scar over his left eye. He was wearing a navy blazer, a white shirt that was open with no tie, and tan slacks. He looked like a businessman that had accidently walked into the ladies' room, not a thug trying to drown a girl in the toilet.

Before he turned to leave, Elliot threw open the door to the ladies' room and took one look at Caleigh on the floor. The look in his eyes, as he whammed his fist across the stranger's face, was murderous. Elliot's face wore rage as the man tried to swing back but was caught in midair by Elliot's left foot knocking the stocky man onto the marble floor. Elliot didn't stop. He slammed two punches in succession at the man before the stocky man could even lift his fist. Elliot stepped his foot across the man's Adam's Apple and applied enough pressure to where the man couldn't breathe.

"You tell your Dexco partners that if they ever come near this young lady, I will personally kill them." Elliot kicked him in the side. He reached down and pulled a gun from his ankle holster. "Now get the hell out of here before I kill you. And take the exit through the kitchen."

The stocky man rolled to his side and gasped for air. He looked pissed, and Caleigh thought he was going to take another swing at Elliot. But he stared at the gun, and stood up and was rapidly out the door.

Elliot turned to Caleigh and lifted her off the ground. "Are you okay?"

"I could use some shampoo, but yeah, I'm okay." She looked in the mirror and was shocked to see her pale face surrounded by her soaked chestnut hair. Her neck had red welts on it where the man had grabbed it.

"Come on. Let's get you to the safe house." Elliot directed her not through the front of the restaurant, but through the kitchen. A few men in chef's aprons glanced up from their meal preparation and back to the food in front of them, like it was an everyday occurrence to cut through the kitchen. There was a large oven with one door open and Caleigh could see a big glass casserole filled with cheesy scalloped potatoes.

"I'll have to try the scalloped potatoes next time," she said to one of the cooks as they hurried past them.

TWENTY-THREE

CALEIGH'S FEAR had so sharply escalated that she stood cold and shivering as they stepped into the back alley.

There was a black ragtop jeep parked by the back door. Elliot opened the passenger side and turned to her. "Get in."

Caleigh jumped in the front passenger seat. Still in a daze from her bathroom swim, she noticed that the driver was a man in his late thirties. He was rugged looking, but handsome.

Elliot shut the door, leaned through the open window, and said, "Caleigh, meet Dice. Dice, this is Ryleigh's twin, Caleigh Lane."

"Hi, Dice," she said as he took her chilled hand into his large warm one.

"Hello, Ms. Caleigh Lane. So nice to finally meet you," Dice said. He had a big genuine smile on his tanned face that made her legs feel weak, and she suddenly wished she had a brush and a blow-dryer.

Elliot asked Dice something about whether they had followed the stocky man from the bathroom. Dice replied that yes, he had a few guys on it. "He'll lead us right to them," Dice said to Elliot, but winked at Caleigh.

"Are you police?" she managed to say to Dice when she finally got her words back.

Dice didn't answer. He just laughed and pulled the jeep from the curb.

"Wait, isn't Elliot coming, too?" She felt a panic coming on as the jeep crept slowly down the dingy alley behind the steak restaurant.

"No," Dice said. And he might have seen her panicked look when he added, "He'll stop by later tonight."

Caleigh leaned back against the car seat. She was exhausted and a bit frightened. She had mixed feelings about what she thought Ashley had told them in the restaurant.

Elliot had said he would have someone hack into Ryleigh's insurance company's mainframe and look at her insurance claims, and get clearance to talk to her doctor. Caleigh had told Elliot that she'd seen a lot of drugs in Ryleigh's cupboards, but she'd thought they were all samples from Ryleigh's company. It had never occurred to her that Ryleigh could be sick. She shivered. Dice turned the heat up in the car and let her sit in silence as he drove through the dark side streets.

They crossed the river at Wacker and traveled through the east side where the restaurants got fewer and fewer, the skyline fainter, and where more houses popped up. She wanted to talk casually to Dice, but she was fighting back tears. Caleigh gritted her teeth, breathing in and out.

She didn't know what to say, so she asked, "Dice, where'd you get that tan?"

He grinned over at her, and said, "I'm from Tampa. I guess from golfing, boating, walking to my car. I try to spend as little time as possible inside."

She nodded, but didn't speak. Caleigh relaxed and decided she liked Dice. He wore dark jeans, a chambray blue shirt, and a brown leather jacket. He had dark brown eyes that were almost black. And his short, dark brown hair had a few graying specks around his sideburns, making him appear probably older than he actually was.

"How are you feeling? Are you warm enough?" Dice asked, glancing her way.

"Yes. Just exhausted."

"I'll have you to the house in less than ten minutes. You can shower and relax. We have your files there and Ryleigh's clothes," he said.

She felt her heart tighten when he mentioned Ryleigh. Poor girl. Alone on an island. And possibly sick. If she had diabetes, was she okay without her insulin?

As if he'd read her mind, he said, "She'll be okay. Elliot is headed there soon. He wants to get to her earlier than planned. He should be to your sister's island in twenty-four to thirty-six hours."

She nodded again and stared out the window. The sun was setting in the sky and a full moon was rising over the horizon. Caleigh watched the bright orange moon and prayed Ryleigh was okay. She wondered what it would be like to stare at the full moon from Ryleigh's beach hideaway. Was that Ryleigh's safe haven? What had happened to Caleigh tonight would have been Ryleigh's fate, had she returned to Chicago. She prayed Ryleigh was safe. Safe and sound.

TWENTY-FOUR
KEG KEY

RYLEIGH ROLLED over on the hammock and watched the wind as it bent the palm trees over almost to the point of snapping. She wanted to hunt for the treasure today, but first the winds needed to die down.

Lying in the hammock, she thought of her life back home. Where would she be? What would she be doing? For years, her life back home had been boring. Predictable. But over the last year, since she had started investigating her employer's intentions with their newly released diabetes drug, life had gotten more exciting.

Then Elliot had entered her life. They'd planned the cruise together, and she'd left with him, almost a stranger in her stateroom. This past month, when she'd had Elliot in her life fulltime, stranded on the island with someone she hardly knew, she'd often wondered what he thought about. He was always so calm. She thought about a lot of things here. She had plenty of time to think.

At times, it was hard for her to beat the beauty and indifference of the island adventure. The only noises came from the fish splashing in the ocean and the waves smashing into the pier near the hut.

Life here was different. Easy, it was not. The atoll of islands' remoteness set it apart from other typical cruise stops. It was an island of poisonous snakes, crabs the size of trash can covers, leaping lizards, and the occasional feral hog – but no humans. She was alone on an island for five more days of doing nothing but surviving.

She saw a flutter of peach and green feathers above her in the palm tree. The parrot was back, and beyond it, fluffy clouds shifted in the sky, transforming to look like images she dreamed about. A boat. A plane. A puppy. A car.

Even as beautiful as the island was, there were times when she hated it. The winding paths and trails that led nowhere; the white, sticky sand that covered everything and every crevasse of her body; the plethora of insects and mosquitos the size of her elbow; greenhead flies that stung like a snake and bees that found nectar in her hair; the deceptively unpredictable weather that had left them stranded on the island which could appear with clear skies one minute, and have a monsoon in the next.

A few days ago, the rain had pelted the hut, and after that when the sun had returned, in a cloudless sky there'd been a huge swarm of insects circling and adhering to its roof. She'd thought the rain would have chased the crawling insects away, but they'd been waterproof and still clinging.

She often heard roars in the island's trees, and screams from its ocean. Sometimes the island was silent. And she had to hum or sing to make sure she was still there.

Ryleigh closed her eyes and the confetti of seagulls circling overhead were vultures waiting to attack, and the strands of seaweed on the beach were poisonous snakes.

"When will you return, Elliot? What if you never do?" She remembered her last few days with Elliot. It had just been last week. When he had told her that she had to stay on the island and hide.

He had said, "If you don't do this, Ryleigh, you'll be looking over your shoulder the rest of your life."

"Can't I hide back in the U.S?" she had pleaded with Elliot.

"No. My pick-up team can't know you're still alive. It's part of the plan. Neither you nor I were supposed to leave the cruise ship, let alone this island, alive. But I got word through the Dexco pirates, and back to my own people in Defense Intelligence, and they agreed to my return. But Dexco has to believe that you're not coming back."

The reality of her being left alone on an uninhabited island for ten days had barely set in when Elliot's helicopter had come for him. Just like that, he was gone. And she was just a girl from Chicago stranded alone on an island.

Before he'd left, they had lived in a perfectly horrible tiki shack near the water. They ate fish, crab, and berries, and drank coconut milk and desalinated water. They ran on the beach, swam with the dolphins, and swatted the mosquitos. And made love.

Now alone on the island, she was on a herculean quest to find herself, a bit of her past and a treasure.

TWENTY-FIVE

SHE MISSED Elliot so much, she thought her heart would burst.

She opened the notebook, and began to scribble. She wrote, *Journal Entry* No ... and then paused. "Hmmm, what number am I on?"

She shrugged and began journaling.

Not much has been done about the food and the water situation. I still have what Elliot left me. It should hold out for five more days. I still can't repair the broken fish station. I talk a lot to my cat. I feel weak, and realize my disease without my meds could be the cause of my fatigue and constant thirst. Why didn't I beg Elliot more, to take me home? I should have been stronger and undermined Elliot's authority. But the question is, what authority? We're not married. We're not even engaged. We barely know each other. Do I roll over and leave it in his hands...?

She laughed aloud. Would this remark garner a sarcastic comment from him... "Yep, roll over baby, and now leave this in my hands, just the way you like it..."

She laughed again. Laughed so hard, she fell out of the hammock, and the notebook fell to the sand. She lay in the sand and thought of Elliot; when she had laughed, he'd told her that she made being stuck on the deserted island easier.

She remembered all the little things he did for her, and what they had done for each other. The last few weeks stranded with Elliot had been special to her, and she should have felt stronger.

Ryleigh stood up and her slim physique cast a long, stalk-like shadow in the sand. She was tall, five-foot-eight when not in heels. She had a slender build, and was extremely well proportioned. Her body had used to be pale – the pale lily of a Chicagoan body, a necrotic stalk.

She often wished she had spent more time at the gym. Island work was tiring. She had worked out occasionally, but was not very athletic. She didn't enjoy running or other strenuous activities and rather do yoga, or calisthenics in front of her DVD in her living room.

As much as she hated to admit it, she had settled her roots into the island, but she missed her living room. Even though she'd hardly ever watched TV, she missed that, too.

She knew Elliot would check in at her place. Make sure everything was in order. She lived alone in Chicago. She lived alone in her world there. With little interaction with other people. She was a girl alone who could do what she wanted, when she wanted.

Despite the strong winds kicking up sand and stirring up algae from the ocean floor, she decided to go for a swim.

She ran into the water, the tantalizing edge of the ocean that frothed far out, and swam in the salty water. The sea was dirtier than she'd ever seen it.

Feeling a chill pass under her, Ryleigh just got this crazy feeling that there was something near her. It was so full of algae that she couldn't clearly see that deep, but she suddenly felt freaked out. She shuddered and swam back toward the beach.

Since being stranded on the island, she had become a stronger swimmer, and this fear in the water was out-of-character, and freaking out was something she just didn't do. But she couldn't explain her sudden fear; she felt like there was a black, gloved hand wrapped around her neck, holding her head under the water. When she submerged, she had a large clump of black seaweed strangling her neck. She swam to shore, struggling for breath.

Ryleigh gasped and gagged and tried to talk, but only squeaky sounds came out. She felt welts on her neck where the critter-laden seaweed algae had been. Her dirty, wet hair framed her face. She lay on the shore, praying for Elliot to return earlier than later. And for some odd reason, she thought of Caleigh, her twin sister.

And for the first time in many years, she prayed Caleigh was safe. Safe and sound.

TWENTY-SIX
THE LAGOON

IT WAS MID-AFTERNOON when the winds died down and she made her way over the hill of flowers toward the lagoon caves. Ryleigh couldn't imagine the indescribable beauty of the gems of scenery that every corner of the island contained.

She continued up the steep climb from the beach, all the while enjoying the incredible views of the shallow turquoise waters below. The rocks were set on the bluff above the beach, and she looked down upon coconut palm trees and Keg Key's pines, which grew so thickly that most of the trails were hidden. The rocks seemed to be suffused in a shimmery green cloud, with lilac and pink flowers everywhere she looked, the sun shining and the temperatures rising.

The flower field always reminded Ryleigh of Elliot. She couldn't exactly remember the name of the flower that grew in marvelous profusion there. She recalled that Elliot had told her it was a native flowering plant that was endemic to the region. She should have raised an eyebrow when he knew the names of many plant species that were only found here and nowhere else in the world. Most men wouldn't have known a chickweed from a hydrangea.

She thought of Elliot and every detail of him. Over the last five days and nights, Ryleigh had recalled the memories of their times together. She could not forget a single detail of Elliot. The way his cloth sheath had worn around the fraying rope belt, exposing his tan, muscular upper thighs. The way he'd always kept his knife laying near the pillow, or the way he'd strapped it into the sheath each morning.

She prayed she was rescued soon because every grain of sand, every shell, and every flower of this wretched island reminded her of him, and drove her crazy with mixed emotions – from hate to pure unadulterated love.

She was thankful for her own discovery of the deep, clear pools off the left side of Keg Key, over a mile from the sandy beach and surrounded by the caves, forming a swimming hole that she had unofficially begun calling "Treasure's Blood."

A clear spring ran into the lagoon with over a 25-foot cascade, so the water was cold and fresh, not salty. If she hadn't found the treasure map that led her to the lagoon spring and waterfall, she may not have survived another few days. She would be found in the tiki hut, dead from boredom.

There was steep, rocky terrain to traverse to get to the Treasure's Blood swimming hole, but she went anyway because she was taking this treasure business pretty seriously – like a woman possessed.

To pass the time on the island, she often picked flowers and fruit, plotted out her escape, fed her cat, and read every symbol on the treasure map, dozens of times over. As she wandered toward the lagoon, she picked the pink, thorny, rose-like flowers.

She bent to gather a flower, and then glanced up and near screamed at seeing a black hog gazing at her. She had the good sense to stay calm and quiet. It snorted and took off in the opposite direction, into a nearby brush by the forest edge.

She felt her knees go weak, and she lay down in the thick flowers, more nervous than usual. With every sound she heard coming from the direction of the forest, she broke out in a cold sweat, thinking it was another wild animal. It never occurred to her that the sounds could be another human being. She had been on the island thirty-nine days, and the only other person who had been there was Elliot. Her home was an uninhabited island that she shared with feral hogs and a stray cat, but no signs of human life.

She sat for a few minutes in the flower field and couldn't feel the beauty of it anymore. She felt trapped. Her days on the tropical island – paradise – were like being incarcerated. Her faded turquoise bikini bottoms, worn with her small novelty t-shirts, were like the orange jumpsuit worn in correctional prisons. The food had become mundane and this, too, felt like she was eating prison food every day.

"Ha, ha," she giggled. "The least of my worries were what to wear each day." Her days were longer here. There was no time wasted for showering and putting on her makeup.

The days on the island were surreal. She didn't think about what clothes to wear. She didn't think about food because she couldn't control what there was to choose from. She ate the stale chips left by the cruise ship, and the bread fruit, coconut, berries, and shell fish, crabs, and other crawling conchs she could easily pluck off the beach. She'd skewer the conch creatures after cracking their shells and roast them over the fire. She'd eaten more fresh fish when Elliot had been there with her to catch it.

Two days after Elliot had left her, the keg that had held the fishing lines had broken loose and floated away. She knew the fishing lines had given Elliot trouble before he'd left, but he'd assured Ryleigh that it would last another few weeks, and it hadn't. The hallow keg floating off had been pretty traumatic. Pieces of the nets had still hung from the side, catching in the undergrowth of seaweed as it rolled out to sea. She had run the length of the beach watching it, and even stepped out into the sea to swim toward it, but gave up. She remembered kicking the beach and swearing as it moved farther and farther from shore. She worried about her constant source of fresh fish.

Spearing fish was difficult for Ryleigh. It took her two days to catch fresh fish. She'd tried to set up a new fishing keg, but she wasn't as smart as Elliot and she had run into more engineering issues every time she attempted to set up the fishing station. She'd worked on it for hours, and barely stopped her work completely that night, and gone to bed from pure exhaustion that evening, still unsuccessful at making a fishing contraption.

This afternoon, she'd hoped to spear fish in the lagoon while she explored the caves. She had never fished so much in her life. Before this trip, the last time Ryleigh had gone fishing, she'd had a Minnie Mouse rod topped off with a worm that her dad had grabbed out of the garden that morning. Now she was here, on an uninhabited island and fishing for food, fishing for her survival. To say she was out of her element would be an understatement.

She was so exhausted and weak most days from her sugar lows, even if she'd found a treasure, she wouldn't have bothered to take it back to the hut. Maybe she would find it and mark the area.

By day forty, she had been stranded away from her medications and been away from the known world for over a month, without any signs of rescue. Without any signs of Elliot.

Although she would not lie around and bitch and mumble about her concerns, she could not hide the anxiety that was building in her. She should have told Elliot about her insulin. She should have told him that the reason she was so concerned about the drug trial was because she had been a victim of her pharmaceutical company's massive cover-up, too.

She kicked at the ground that was carpeted in island flowers, mangrove lilies, and alyssum. Everywhere she looked, small lizards sprinted across the plush path. She also worried about the snakes. It was one of her biggest fears. She had been bitten once, but she'd survived it. She hated the caves where the snakes hid, and only went there during bad storms.

The flower field opened up bright and sweet before her, and the sea in the distance was mirror flat under lambent island sunshine. She saw rows and rows of the flowering bushes, and knew that she was close to the cave lagoon and would be there in less than ten minutes.

There was a brown heap of clothing peeking through the green and pink foliage on the side of the hill. "How did that get there?" Or could it be something else? She felt she was hallucinating. A mirage? Clothes?

She caught sight of it and then it was gone, covered by the windy bushes. She veered off her path to investigate it. She had to. She couldn't let it go.

That's when she saw it. The still, dark brown mound on the side of the hill wasn't a pile of clothes, and it wasn't a feral hog – it was human. It was another person. A man.

TWENTY-SEVEN
THE SAFE HOUSE

THE droning noise of the Jeep's engine comforted Caleigh as they left behind the built-up metro areas of Chicago and moved just beyond the outskirts of town on bumpy back streets.

Staring out the window, she caught a glimpse of her reflection. Although she had been up for almost 24 hours and her semi-wet hair was plastered to her head, her pale face looked bright and a natural pink glow flushed her cheeks. Her wet hair was drying in long, loose curls. She sank back in the leather seats, relaxing.

"I've been away farming sheep too long. This city life is a real killer," she said, breaking the silence.

It was dark in the jeep, but as Dice turned toward her, she could still make out his features. Although Dice had told her earlier that he had just crossed the threshold into his forties, he still looked as if he was in his early thirties, like herself. His sand-colored hair showed a slight trace of grey; his handsome, brown-eyed face bore few if any lines, and his over-six-foot body was in better physical shape than those of men half his age. To see the toll his career in special ops had taken, one would have to look elsewhere, because Dice was a sexy man. He could have been a cover model for GQ, versus her bodyguard for the night.

"Yes, certainly, areas of the city are more dangerous than most places," he said, alternating glances back at her and the rear-view mirror.

"I like it." She smiled over at him, eyeing him and trying her best to flirt.

He shook his head, but didn't reply.

"What?" Caleigh asked. "I like the city."

"It's just that I feel like I already know you." He had a quirk in his cheeks like he knew a secret joke. "You look so much like Ryleigh."

"You knew her well?" She hadn't realized Dice had known her twin sister.

"I knew of her. I studied her a lot, preparing for this operation. I did meet her once, but she didn't know who I was."

"So you watched her?" Caleigh shivered slightly.

"Like a bodyguard. She wasn't even aware of it." Dice reached over and adjusted the vent.

"I often wondered what she was like – today, I mean." She leaned back, and warmth from the vent uncurled within her.

"I caught glimpses of Ryleigh at the restaurants around her work and saw her pictures in the files, so I had an impression of her, but being in this car with you... it's as if she's sitting right here. Your mannerisms, and body language, and of course your looks are identical from what I can see. Even your, I mean Ryleigh's, ex-employer sees you as her, too."

"I'm not surprised to hear it. That's why I felt confident and agreed to be the witness at the trial. I knew Ryleigh hadn't changed a lot." She paused, not sure how much she should share with him.

"I came to the city once," she continued.

Dice looked over at her. He raised his eyebrows, more curious than surprised, but he didn't say a word.

"It was about a year and a half ago. I told myself I was here for a large farm convention. It was in Decatur," she recalled. "But I stayed close to her townhouse. I watched her come and go, but I couldn't bring myself to make the move to contact her." She felt a pain inside. "Now I wish I would have."

"It's okay. You being here now and agreeing to get caught up in this trial mess is going to be a special surprise to her."

Caleigh looked at Dice, and she saw the empathy in his eyes. The understanding. He knew why she'd decided to do this, and he wasn't judging her.

He had an amazing smile. "I hope I can pull it off and my testimonial helps tomorrow. I'm worried that I'll still be stalked, too." She glanced in the side mirror.

"No doubt your presence today was quite the surprise that caused an alarm within Dexco," he said. "Our team will make sure the guy that came after you won't be coming around. But we need to be careful, Ry–" he stopped and corrected himself, "–Caleigh. Sorry."

"It's okay. I'm used to it. When I was here last year, a few of her neighbors recognized me as Ryleigh, at the coffee shop I visited close to her place. It brought back memories of our childhood and growing up together. We were so close."

She looked over at his hands, wrapped around the steering wheel. "I need to see Ryleigh. I want closure and to be a part of her life again." It felt comfortable talking to Dice.

He stopped the car in front of a dark, two-story brick building. She took in the dilapidated state of the building and thought, *if this is a safe house, I'd be better off taking my chances at my cousin's condo in Naperville.*

The double wood doors were painted in what had probably once been white, but was now grey, with patches of paint worn or missing, and the windows had small cracks in the glass and missing panes here and there.

"Are we here?" she asked.

"Yes. Let me show you the way."

Dice exited the jeep and came around to the passenger side, opening the door. He helped her out and grabbed the duffle from the back seat.

He grabbed her hand, and it was comforting to feel a warm, strong hand leading her through a maze of pavement alleys. They took a sidewalk leading behind the brick building.

It became clear to her that the building in front of them wasn't actually the safe house as he led her around the back and across a back garden, where she could see a slightly more flattened area that made a long path. The garden was overgrown and a cobweb stretched across two trees, moving slightly in the cold breeze. She brushed it away so that it wouldn't get caught in her hair. There was a rock pathway leading down and away from the back of the building, and a gate opening at the end of the path, leading to a dirt track road.

They crossed through the open gate, and Dice shut the squeaky iron door behind them. The clanging of the gate latches gave her a chill.

"Thank goodness there's a full moon or I don't know how you'd find this path."

"Shhh," he said, placing his finger over his lips.

She quieted and felt a cool shiver run over her.

They walked further down the dirt road, and she heard a scurry in the brush. In an instant, without a word, Dice pulled his gun from his shoulder holster. An act that Caleigh had seen on TV, but never in front of her. She held her breath, tensing all her muscles throughout her upper body, frozen in place.

The movement in the brush got closer and closer, and her imagination was rampant. *What if it's the man from the lady's room? Returning to finish the job?*

She sucked in a silent breath and tried not to panic. Her damp hair and the cool air chilled her, and all she could do was pray her teeth wouldn't chatter.

The brush rustled in front of her and her knees buckled; she fell to all fours.

PAMELA LAUX MOLL

TWENTY-EIGHT

FROM HER SQUATTING position, Caleigh saw the intruder emerge. A large raccoon darted out, and scurried across the path and into another cluster of bushes, never looking in their direction.

She felt the tension drain from her body and she practically melted into the path of dead leaves mixed with pine needles. She breathed a heavy sigh of relief, but as she stood up her knees began to tremble uncontrollably. *Damn it. I'm a tough girl, and a little varmint in the woods isn't going to make me pass out.*

Dice came to her side, and helped her up and guided her for a few seconds. His cell vibrated and he answered it.

"Yes. Raccoon," he said softly, and clicked off his phone.

"Who's watching us?" Caleigh whispered in his ear, enjoying his manly smells, and trying to sound calm and not totally helpless.

"The team. From the building."

"They can see all the way back here?"

"No. Infrared."

"Oh." She wondered how his team could have seen them if the rustle in the bushes had been her assailant. But then, with their thermal imaging cameras, she was sure they saw two tall red figures walking to the house, two humans. If they would have seen three, it would have been another story. How long had they been watching them? Had they followed them here? Once she was settled in the safe house, she wanted answers. She knew the big picture was important here, and Caleigh wanted to know what that was.

They came out of the brushy path and into the clearing where there sat a small, two-story wood house, and standing on a large wrap-around porch was Elliot, talking quietly with another man. She felt instant relief and, beyond that, she suddenly felt safe. Very safe.

"Hi, Caleigh," Elliot said. "How are you feeling?"

"Better," she said, smiling. And now she knew how Ryleigh had lived alone on an island for a month with this man. Now Caleigh just needed to find out why Ryleigh had agreed to stay there. The big picture.

They settled into the living room of the painted dark green house. The cottage at the end of the damp, pine-needled lane was just fifteen miles from Chicago. She was told it had lain derelict for ten years before the agency had purchased it and the red brick building, and renovated the property into a safe house compound. The first floor held the hallway, the kitchen, the living room, and a small den. The ground floor windows were covered with special wire that couldn't be penetrated. Bullet proof. But one couldn't tell by looking at them. From all appearances, it looked and felt like a cottage in the woods.

The second floor held the main bedroom and bathroom, guest bedroom and bathroom, and an office.

The house was modern and comfortable, and it reminded her of a summer cottage home on a lake.

"Are you okay?" Elliot asked. "If you're up for it, we'll talk more about tomorrow's trial, and then I need to head out." He wore a confident I-don't-worry-about-a-thing, worrying-about-everything look in his eyes.

"I'm fine, we've covered everything already. Do you have ibuprofen?" she asked, rubbing the fading red marks on her neck.

Elliot nodded to Dice. Dice left the living room, and returned with a tall glass of water and handed Caleigh a bottle.

She shook out four ibuprofens and dumped them down her throat, following them with a long drink of the cold water. "Thank you."

"Are you warm enough? Hungry?" Dice guided Caleigh toward the couch. "Relax. I'll make a fire."

"What I'd really like is a shower." Her hair felt saturated with toilet conditioner. "Then we can talk."

Dice's lips pursed and he suddenly looked rather formidable, less affable. "Of course. There are towels under the sink, and you should find pajamas or sweats, whatever you're most comfortable with, upstairs." Dice bent over the fireplace and lit a few of the logs with a long wooden match.

She walked over to him and put her hand on his shoulder, catching him by surprise. "Thank you," she said.

Elliot had his back to them, looking at his phone.

On impulse, she bent over and kissed Dice's cheek, and before she could see his reaction, Caleigh turned and went toward the stairs in search of a hot shower.

TWENTY-NINE

ELLIOT FINN STOOD in the living room of the safe house, shaking his head. "Caleigh, I've shared everything I know about it."

Since he'd left Caleigh at the restaurant with Dice, he had made a dozen phone calls, and it was true, Ryleigh was sick. She had adult onset type 1 diabetes, a disease that needed medications. She would be fine overall in life, but she needed to take her meds every day. Shots of insulin.

He recalled the recent phone conversation with the doctor. Elliot had talked to him on the drive over to the safe house.

"Dr. Staub?" Elliot had realized he was holding his breath while he rolled through the questions and listened to the doctor's answers. He knew Dr. Staub had been given clearance and ordered to give Elliot what he asked.

Elliot listened and barely responded, and his voice trailed off, swallowing hard as he continued to gaze at the dreary, cold, gray world beyond the car window.

He barely held the cell to his ear as an image barged into his mind, of the crystal blue sea. He sucked in a deep breath, expecting to smell salt air and Ryleigh's sunscreen; sometimes that happened. Not this evening.

He could only see the water. He couldn't smell it, or hear the crashing waves. Something had risen from the blue-black depths in the distance, just beyond the rocks. A fin. A shark? He saw Ryleigh nearby, floating on the inner tube, too weak from her disease to swim, to fight.

"Elliot?" A voice distracted him, and he blinked his eyes, too worried to listen any further.

"Thank you, doctor. Yes, I promise to keep her on the insulin shots." He hung up the phone and made a note to get the insulin pens and prescriptions that she needed, and add them to the brown Louis Vuitton sitting on his backseat.

Ryleigh had been a very courageous woman, to deal with this alone. She'd had the guts to stay behind on an uninhabited island, against her nature, and to hide out while Elliot uncovered Dexco's scam and crimes.

Elliot sank into the car seat, the words of Dr. Staub rolling around in his head. The doctor had asked; *did she take her insulin every day? Does she test her blood? Is she eating the right foods? If she doesn't take care of herself, she's going to die.*

Well, all right, the doctor hadn't really told Elliot that last thing. But Elliot had thought it, all the time the doctor was talking to him. He worried about Ryleigh every day. He worried about shark attacks, pirates, Dexco, drowning, and snake bites, but the thought of a disease scared him. He shouldn't have had to think about her dying from a disease. She was a young, beautiful person, inside and out. When he thought of Ryleigh, his insides melted.

The doctor had said that many chronic diseases are not treatable, but that diabetes was, and the treatments had Ryleigh taken were better than any others. He had mentioned that Dexco Pharmaceuticals had had a break-through drug, one of the fastest advancements in the medical field.

Words rang in Elliot's brain, "you can't ignore diabetes, or it kills you."

She could get tired and pass out when her blood sugar got too low. Hadn't Ryleigh passed out a few times when they'd first been stranded on the island?

Dr. Staub had said that if she stepped on a nail or hurt her foot in some way, that infection might set in faster with low blood sugar. Gangrene could set in.

Sweetheart, I had no idea! I'm coming for you, Ryleigh.

He now knew why she'd wanted to take down Dexco. It hadn't just been her intentions of revenge, but to protect so many innocent people. Enough that he wondered if she didn't know what he had planned. It hurt his heart to think about it. The best he could do now was to finish the job.

"Elliot, are you listening to me?" Caleigh asked, bringing him back in to the conversation.

"Yes. Damn, why didn't she tell me?"

"Don't agonize over it. You couldn't have known. She hid it well."

"But my agency did their due diligence. But you're right, she covered it up well. She went to someone inside the company, one of their doctors on staff. She did everything internally within the confines of Dexco, and all under the radar." Elliot's worry mounted with every second he thought of Ryleigh being left alone on the island.

Without her in his life, he felt his world had been drained of all he enjoyed and loved. His life had had more meaning and color when stranded alone together with her. He had spent the last five days and nights dreaming of her. And now, here in Chicago, he had to face the identical, but slight variation of Ryleigh.

He was in the living room of the safe house with Ryleigh Lane's identical twin, Caleigh He had always known about Caleigh

Lane. She had been part of the plan from the beginning. What he hadn't realized was how hard it would be, seeing Caleigh, and how much she reminded him of Ryleigh.

He had scarcely been able to eat or think in the steak restaurant because he had stared into those identical emerald eyes with golden brown flecks. Thank God, Ryleigh's friend had distracted them.

He looked out the window to the covered porch and saw Dice talking to Denny, the night watchman.

"What are you going to do? Do you have her insulin to take with you? What else is going on? I feel like I'm not understanding the full importance of this mission." Caleigh asked.

"My God, this is like talking to Ryleigh," he said with a smile. "Not just your looks and mannerisms, but the endless questions."

"I'm just shocked that Ryleigh really has diabetes. This plan has been compromised now. It was so dangerous leaving her there anyway. I never agreed to that part of the plan. You need go get her immediately." Caleigh was twisting her wet hair, a gesture Ryleigh had done often when in a heated discussion with him.

"I am going to her. I fly out tonight. As soon as Ashley told us about Ryleigh's sickness, I made arrangements." It was true. He was going to skip the trial and leave that in Dice's hands. If only he had convinced the powers-to-be to delay the seismic testing in that region for a few days. He worried and wondered if Dexco was behind the earth vibration theory, then why even do it? If they thought Ryleigh was alive and well in Chicago, and not stranded on the island, why cause the earthquakes? He had an idea, but felt these other reasons couldn't be discussed yet.

THIRTY

"CAN YOU SHARE with me more about the drug mess Ryleigh has gotten into?" Caleigh asked, not letting up on the ten-minute conversation. She wore gray sweatpants, an oversized cable knit, white sweater, and her long chestnut hair was still wet from her shower, fanned across her back with a few loose strands falling in her face.

"It's complicated," Elliot said.

"I like complicated."

"We're investigating more than a drug company cover-up."

"We?"

He smiled at her, and walked over from the fireplace and placed his hand on the top of her shoulder. She smelled of baby powder and ivory soap. "You know I can't."

"Come on, Elliot. I know you and Dice are some secret operatives. I really don't care whether you're CIA, or FBI, or DIA, or any other three letter acronym affiliation. It's none of my concern. I just want to know that my sister will be safe after my testimony tomorrow. That she can come back here and live her life without looking over her shoulder all the time."

"Yes, that's the plan. As trials go, if there are no bombshells or surprises, it will conclude quickly after your testimony uncovers the internal documents and Dexco's cover-up. After all evidence indicates Dexco, that will begin their demise. It may open the door for homicide investigations."

"If they murdered innocent people for the sake of money, and profit, I can see why you kept her away. When can I see her?"

"I'll pick up Ryleigh day after tomorrow, a few days earlier than planned. She'll be back here by Saturday, and all will be good." He felt a small jolt in his heart. Would Ryleigh return home, here? What would she think of Elliot after being intentionally left alone for a week on an uninhabited island?

"Why do I feel like you're not sharing everything with me?" Caleigh asked.

Elliot felt a déjà vu, as if it was Ryleigh six days earlier, sitting on the rock at the end of the beach, saying those exact words, holding his knife in her clenched hand. He had lied to Ryleigh to protect her. Tonight, he had to do the same with Caleigh. He needed to tell Caleigh enough to get her on the stand tomorrow and confidently tell the testimony they had rehearsed.

"My job is to make sure the jurors are persuaded by your carefully chosen words, without you trying to twist it."

Caleigh looked thoughtful and somewhat heartfelt, but she wasn't buying everything. Just like Ryleigh.

He wanted to make sure Caleigh was ready, and that she got a good night's sleep. Her expression on her face was that of Ryleigh's ghost, a doppelganger there with him.

"I'm ready. I don't think I need to rehearse again."

"Okay then. You should get some rest. 9:00 AM will be here fast. Why don't you review your notes and get to bed? You'll do fine. You have your intellect and common bond with Ryleigh." He faced Caleigh and touched her shoulders with his hands. "I'm proud of both of you."

He stared at her, waiting for a gesture or a comment like Ryleigh would have made. His brain felt muddled by her close presence and by the equal likeness, and he resisted an urge to push the wet stray strands of hair from her face. Backing up, he didn't trust himself to look into those emerald-Ryleigh-like eyes.

He watched Caleigh's eyes brighten a little in understanding, and her faint smile.

"You're right, maybe I should go to bed," she said. "I'm exhausted."

Why had he released a sigh of relief? Was he relieved not to have to lie to her? Like he had Ryleigh?

"Thank you, Caleigh, for doing this. You're a lifesaver."

"I'm doing this not only for Ryleigh, but for all the other people with diabetes whose lives are at risk. And if Greg Edersom, the Dexco CEO, gets away with this, then what's next? What's stopping him?"

It had been a tough choice to do this mission. Over the last thirteen months, Elliot had been watching Ryleigh, a little too closely. What had started out as investigating Dexco Pharmaceuticals, through his relationship with Ryleigh, had turned into a full-blown cover-up and protecting the star witness.

If it had been a simple choice between Elliot's own safety or Ryleigh's, he wouldn't have hesitated at all. From the start, the day he'd met her, it had seemed unthinkable to him to put Ryleigh in danger for any reason whatsoever. But it wasn't that simple. It wasn't even a matter of it being his decision, in the long run. The agency had made that clear.

He recalled when he had reached out to Caleigh. "I'm going to go through with this," Elliot had said, "whether you help or not. Dexco has to be stopped. And you can help. You're our best chance at nailing these murderers. Dice and I talked it over, and we can train you, Caleigh, on how to expose them. We know they'll make sure Ryleigh isn't let off that island, alive. We can make her comfortable enough there, out of the way, while you sneak into Chicago without any suspicion."

"But what if you're wrong? And they find me out? Or someone finds Ryleigh during the next week?" Caleigh had asked a lot of questions before agreeing.

"If we're wrong, then we go to Plan B. But if we're right, then a silent killer's loose, whose CEO thinks he can get away with murder whenever he feels like it. So many innocent people were in a deadly drug study. Many will die from cardiac arrest or other natural causes brought on by the Dexco drugs."

"Can we confront them? Call them out?"

"Unfortunately, no. Greg is an arrogant but cautious CEO, and he's gone to great lengths to cover this up. He's decided it's a lot cheaper to get rid of Ryleigh at all costs, than to come out with the truth and withdraw the drug. God knows what he may think. A killer's thinking is all twisted and confused."

Caleigh had paused, and looked long and thoughtfully at Elliot. "I will do this. Because Ryleigh is a strong girl and she went through a lot as a child and teenager. I know she can handle this plan, too. She has a lot of courage." Caleigh had told him.

"Elliot, are you okay?"

"Sorry, I just saw someone coming down the path." He stood at the living room window for another minute, and then turned and saw a look of panic cross Caleigh's face.

"It's fine. It's Josh coming to spell Denny." He knew that every few hours they would take turns warming up in the building.

Dice, who had been in the kitchen, entered the living room.

"Is everything okay in here?" Dice asked.

Elliot noticed Caleigh's stare and locked on to Dice's eyes as he walked over to the dying fire, removing his jacket while reaching for the iron poker. One thing Elliot had caught about Dice's movements was the way he glanced back at Caleigh. Something was there. He wasn't sure what it was, but it was something special. A special emotion. Special agents controlled their emotions, not the other way around.

"We were chatting about tomorrow's trial," Elliot said.

After Dice finished tweaking the fire, he settled on a brown leather loveseat alongside Caleigh, and before the three launched into a discussion, Elliot saw the lingering look the two gave each other.

"I know this is going to be one of the hardest things you've ever done, Caleigh, but we're here for you," Dice said.

Elliot heard genuine concern in Dice's voice and a hint of trying to win her attention. He shook his head.

THIRTY-ONE
CHICAGO SUBURB

CHANDLER KEPT his head slumped as he spun back to consciousness. When he opened his eyes, his view was blocked by a loosely-tied black fabric. Through the bottom of the blindfold, he could see his ankles were wrapped with a rope and pinned to the legs of a wooden folding chair. His wrists were bound together behind his back.

His head ached and he needed a cigarette. Maybe he should feign unconsciousness as long as he could, in order to assess the situation around him.

He wiggled his fingers and felt the rope across his wrists. The rope wrapped across his chest and bulging midsection, and moved slightly when he pushed forward.

He heard an unfamiliar man's muffled voice in the next room, which he presumed was the garage behind the house he'd tried to enter. He heard squeaky footsteps, followed by the sounds of a cheap aluminum door banging behind the person as they entered the room.

"Look who's coming around," the man's voice said.

Chandler tried to recognize the voice, but he had no clue who it was. It didn't seem to be the same guy who had tied him to the chair and blindfolded him.

"What the hell is going on here?" Chandler asked. And then guttural noises came from his throat, from the lingering effects of the chloroform they'd used to put him out. He took small breaths with every sentence.

The blindfold was loose enough to see under it as the man stood directly in front of the chair. His captor had a little Colt .25 automatic in his hand, the metal's sheen flickering from the glow of blue lighting. Blue lights that were common in dark garages.

"Who are you? What do you want? I think there's been a mistake."

"No, Mr. Chandler. There's no mistake. We brought you here to discuss what you know about the girl on the island."

"Who's we?" Chandler wasn't sure what this man was talking about, and he didn't like his tone.

"That's not your business."

"I think it is. You've kidnapped me, tied and blindfolded me, so that makes it my business." Chandler could see the man's large, brown, tasseled shoes moving directly in front of the chair. He felt the cold steel of the butt of the gun against his cheek and the same familiar smell of this guy's body odor, which Chandler had gotten a whiff of before he'd eaten bricks.

"Just answer my questions."

Geez. What had Chandler gotten into? Had he gotten soft in his detective days? As a cop, he would have never walked into the situation he had been in earlier without back-up. And a plan.

And possibly another weapon. Even if he had hidden a knife, though, his kidnappers would have found it.

"What questions do you have? And can we lose the blindfold?"

"Come on, detective. Just answer me. Is the girl dead or alone on the island, or maybe she escaped?"

Chandler was still part-time investigating the missing cruise passengers lost at sea, but what was this goon looking for? Why were he and Elliot worrying about this girl? What about the island, Keg Key?

"What do I get if I tell you?"

The guy didn't answer, but he slammed Chandler's left cheek. Hard.

Shit. What did Chandler have to lose? Why not talk a little? He was probably a dead man anyway. Whoever had brought him here wouldn't just drop him off on his merry way. He might as well share some of what he knew.

"You mean the girl from the cruise ship?" Chandler could still play detective before they silenced him forever.

"Yes. The Lane girl."

Chandler wasn't at a complete loss, as a trained ex-cop. He had learned a lot through his interrogation days.

In his semi-conscious state, Chandler had taken precautions. He had recalled that, when they knocked him out earlier, they'd dragged him into the body shop behind the garage in the run-down neighborhood. When they'd tied him up, he had positioned his body carefully when the ropes were secured. He had crossed his hands behind his back and flexed his muscles as much as possible, without the goon knowing what he was doing.

Chandler had appeared barely conscious, while all the time he'd been getting tied up, he'd kept moving an undetectable dance, a half inch here and there. Which would come in handy when he wasn't tense and the ropes could loosen up.

He had rolled his shoulders forward and breathed in as deeply as he could, expanding his chest to its fullest. Making the rope across his chest tight when the goon had strapped him to the chair, but loose when he let the air out.

He talked in short, shallow breaths, making sure not to let out all of his air. "Take my blindfold off and I'll tell you what I know about her." He couldn't even remember her first name. Was it Rhonda? Ruth?

"Are you threatening me?" The loafer shoe goon moved closer to Chandler.

"Look, this isn't necessary. I'll tell you what you want. I have no reason to hide anything. Whoever you work for is going to unusual measures for free information."

"Free?"

"I usually get paid pretty well for my detective work, but in this case, I won't charge." Chandler wanted to get the questioning done so the goon would leave the small room. He knew that if he could be alone he'd be able to take off his loose boots and slide his feet out of the ropes. He planned to stand up and break the chair to free his hands.

The cramped space smelled like oil and lime. Automobile grease and oil and lime soap to clean it off the goon's hands. What were these expensive tasseled loafers doing in a grease monkey shop? Those shoes belonged in a boardroom, a pharmaceutical company's boardroom. If he was to take his captor seriously, those shoes weren't cutting it. They didn't make a sense of alarm run through him. The idea that Dexco Pharmaceuticals would kidnap a detective... now, that set off alarms.

THIRTY-TWO

CHANDLER JUST NEEDED to be alone. He would make these ropes look like child's play. The blindfold was a good sign. That usually meant kidnappers didn't plan to kill their captives.

"Well, you're going to give us the information about Ryleigh, the girl on the cruise. You've been investigating her. Why? Who sent you to do that? And what do you know?"

Ryleigh? Aha, so that's her name.

"Truth is, I'm just an insurance company detective. I was hired to make sure the passengers and employees that drowned and disappeared on the cruise are who they say they are. There's a lot of money in insurance claims, and fraud is prevalent." Chandler hoped he'd given enough information to placate the guy, but still not show all his cards.

"And what did you discover? About the girl? Is she dead?"

"Looks that way." He took a stab in the dark and hoped he'd given him what he wanted to hear.

"That's good, my employers, anyway, will be happy. How do you know for sure? I need to know everything you've found out."

Chandler recalled he had investigated Ryleigh Lane and run into some dead ends. But this guy didn't need to know that. He didn't think he needed to tell the Dexco goon that two of Ryleigh's neighbors had made a bona fide direct spotting of her, and even come in contact with her a few weeks ago. They claimed to have talked to her at a nearby coffee shop. The elderly couple had verified it was her, and that she was fine and well. Would Dexco have discovered this, too?

"I know she was last seen on the excursion island. What's the name, Keg Key?"

"Yeah, go on."

"There's great history surrounding that island. Did you know there's been rumors for centuries that there's a hidden treasure on it? And yet, not many people know this." Chandler felt the guy was relaxing.

"Treasure? That's crap."

"The island is covered with caves. There could be a real Indiana Jones treasure buried there." Chandler wiggled his hands, crossed behind his back ever so lightly, so no movement would be detected from directly in front of him. "Maybe that Ryleigh girl is a treasure hunter and she stayed behind because she's searching for it."

"Why do you think that?" He came closer to the chair, and for a moment Chandler was worried he'd caught on to his hand movements behind his back.

Chandler heard a bit of excitement and irritation in the man's voice, and as he drew closer, he could see his loafers through the bottom slit of an opening in the blindfold. The Brits like to say you can judge a man by his shoes. In his gut, he didn't think this guy was a killer. He could also see the man's gun was back in his shoulder holster. This could be a good sign. His kidnapper was lightening up.

"I'm pretty thirsty. Do you think I can have some water, before I share everything?"

"I'll get you water, but when I get back, you need to do more talking or else."

Another good sign, Chandler thought. We're having a drink together. As soon as the door slammed shut, Chandler wiggled the rope off of his midsection. Moving rapidly, he shifted his feet until his shoes came off, which allowed him to pull his ankles and feet free.

He leaned forward, stood, and then tipped the chair to the side, quietly toppling it to the floor. He slipped out of the ropes that held him to the chair, rolled over, and got to his feet and stood, with his hands still bound behind his back. He heard muffled sounds outside the door and his heart started to thud – a heart-attack pain that he couldn't dampen.

He raised his hands up as far as he could, to his shoulder blades, pushing his chest forward.

"Shit," he murmured as he tucked in his thumbs and slid his hands away from each other.

The ropes dropped away and his hands slithered free, just as he heard footsteps. He whipped the blindfold off and spun around to see the loafered kidnapper opening the door. He would get his gun and kill him. He'd rather be tried by a jury of twelve than buried six feet under.

Chandler dove forward and smashed the door against the man's face, and he and two bottles of water went flying across the garage floor.

"What the fuck!" the man yelled, groping at his shoulder holster for his gun.

Chandler knew the next few moments would be crucial. His surprise attack had made the man on the floor ill-prepared for Chandler's suddenly aggressive move.

He punched him across the bridge of his nose, and in return he felt a forceful blow to the side of his neck. Strong arms wrestled him and pulled Chandler to the ground. Chandler rolled on top of the man and grabbed at the gun.

They both wrestled with the Colt – and boom! – the gun went off.

Chandler felt a hot burn in his chest.

He heard the fading sound of the man lying under him, "I don't believe you know what you got yourself into and know who you're dealing with."

"Fuck you," Chandler moaned. And then he added in a raspy voice, "In the future, if you want to be taken seriously and more threatening, I'd change your footwear."

The man lying under him emitted a soft, throaty laugh and then pushed Chandler's body off of him and onto the greasy garage floor.

THIRTY-THREE
THE FLOWER FIELDS NEAR THE LAGOON

RYLEIGH RAN TOWARD the man who was lying face down just beyond the low rows of hydrangea bushes on the hillside.

She fell to her knees and touched the man. He felt cool to the touch, and when she rolled him over, she knew the dark eyes staring at her were those of a dead man. Ryleigh had never seen a dead person. He was unnaturally stiff. All the life had run out of him. A single arrow protruded from his chest. She leaned in to listen to his breathing, and she heard nothing.

He was a young man, maybe in his twenties. His body was coconut brown tan and his dark hair was long to his shoulders. This bearded man looked familiar. Was he from the cruise ship? He wore brown cargo shorts and a white t-shirt that said *Captain* on the small pocket with an anchor underneath it. A torn package of cigarettes was protruding from the pocket. A red ring of blood circled around the wound in his chest.

Her eyes caught some movement of a shadow just over the hill. It was crazy, but she thought she saw a young girl. A female? She sunk low near the stiff body. She didn't need to take his pulse because rigor mortis had crept into his muscles around his eyes, mouth, and jaw, and his fingers were balled stiffly together on his right hand, awkwardly closed like a fist. A piece of paper stuck out from between his fingers.

She knew that it was a high risk move to be out there in the open.

She saw a flash of brown in the air making a streak past her. There was the sound of a snap like a twig falling nearby, and she saw the arrow as it chopped off the blossoms of three flowers before piercing the ground by her left foot.

"Oh my God." *Somebody shot an arrow at me!* Because of the angle of the hill and the brushy flower bushes, she couldn't see the other person near her.

She felt a strong snake bite type of pain in her foot, and bent over to examine it. There was an arrow that looked like a bamboo reed stuck dead center in the middle of her foot. Yelling out in pain, she grasped at the white feathered shaft. She tugged on it, and piercing agony shot through her foot, a small rivulet of blood appearing around the puncture wound. She breathed in deep, making small groaning sounds.

It occurred to her that she was a sitting duck, and whoever had shot that arrow and killed the man next to her could be at her side any second.

The native man next to her seemed to move, as she now half knelt near him, with the contraction of rigor over brittle bones or maggots under his skin and in his innards. Her mind was racing.

She had to hide and decided the place to do that was in the caves by the lagoon. Before she took off, she used gentle pressure on the dead man's fingers and removed the paper. His body felt warm still, but stiff. Dead for three hours or so?

By the sheer force of fear, she moved, stumbling across the path, scanning as she went. No one that she could see. Looking at the brown heap of death on the ground, she was startled at the sight of another human. A dead one!

If she attempted a one legged run for the lagoon and the caves, her chances of making it would be slim, but at least there would be a hope that she could hide from the arrow murderer.

Her face knitted in pain and washed of color, she felt on the verge of nausea. She shook her foot and rubbed her swollen toes, the color of blueberry stains.

Swearing softly, she kept going, placing her good foot in front of her. Her eyes scanned all around her, and as she took a few steps, she tripped over a fallen palm throng, and suddenly she started to tumble down the hill. The world spun in front of her. Her right shoulder slammed into the sandy soil of flowers as she heard the sickening popping sound of the bamboo arrow snapping off, and sharp fingers of pain shooting up her right leg.

THIRTY-FOUR

RYLEIGH GRIMACED at the grotesque mess of her foot. The force of her fall had twisted her arrowed ankle in an odd direction. Rolling onto her side, she tried standing gingerly as she struggled to put pressure on her right ankle. She could feel the pain with each step she attempted. She managed to hop a few steps, lost her balance, and fell forward, her face planted into the pink flowers.

The dual pain from her shot ankle and the shock from seeing the dead man began to spin in her head. She crawled, dragging herself through the ever-deepening flowery brush. She made a futile attempt to reach the lagoon and shelter, but the odds of reaching it before dark were nonexistent. The thought of spending the night in the flower field, surrounded by dense forest and brush that could harbor a murderer, kept her pushing forward. She tried to stand again and the pain was excruciating.

Her vision began to blur from the tears in her eyes and she screamed into the hillside, knowing there was no one there to hear her, except maybe the dead man's murderer. She had never known so much fear before.

"If I can just make it back to the caves, I could stay the night there," she said to herself, encouraging her efforts.

She stood and hobbled a few more steps toward the lagoon. The beginnings of the sunset fell across the water as her head began to feel light, and the first signs of fatigue and unconsciousness coiled around her brain.

She managed to make it down the flower hill, but the pain in her ankle permeated her leg and she called out once again, "Elliot," as blackness enveloped her, and she closed her eyes. She just needed to lie there a few minutes by the lagoon before wading in the water to the caves behind the waterfalls.

She glanced at the paper in her hand and read on one side: *Good Luck Skipper Trevor, Love Lilah.*

Ryleigh turned it over and saw a map. A treasure map? *Trevor? Lilah? That's right!* The dead man was Trevor, the captain of the ferry boat from the cruise ship. Lilah was the cruise ship coordinator. A thrill of excitement passed through her when she realized the cruise ship people were back on the island. She was finally going to be rescued.

Driven by a sudden burst of energy, she stuffed the map into her sheath and tried to pull herself up again. The pain was excruciating and her insides were fuzzy. She felt a stinging sensation in her head and a nauseous feeling in her stomach. She sank half-conscious into the flowers. *Was the arrow poisonous?*

There was a shadow standing over her. She could see a turned down, blurred face, but couldn't make out any features. A sudden vertigo snapped her eyes out of focus and she could see two of them. Two blurred figures. Tiredness swept through her. She blinked her eyes.

Just a few minutes. She closed her eyes, and saw no more.

THIRTY-FIVE

RYLEIGH DRIFTED IN and out of consciousness in a field of flowers. She was angry and livid at Elliot, angry and livid at herself for allowing Elliot to leave her here. Now she was lying in a field of hydrangea with an arrow protruding from her foot. She wanted Elliot to be here by her side, fighting the arrow shooter. He had saved her so many times before; from hunger, from sharks, from insanity. She remembered her Hunk-a-berry Finn and how he had always saved her. She remembered like he was there in front of her.

"What happened to that sweet girl I met?" Elliot asked.

"Sweet stops after two weeks of no hot water for a shower and no real food to eat."

"Be nice. You have all the fresh seafood you could eat." Elliot took pleasure in pulling the crab leg from its shell, rinsing it in the salty sea they stood in, before handing it to her.

"I'm tired of being the nice girl. I stopped being nice after the cruise ship left us alone with no return to the mainland." Ryleigh swallowed the pink, slimy shell fish limb, without a blink, in one bite.

He pried another large hunk of crabmeat from its body and placed it on her tongue.

Between bites, she garbled, "I'm not trying to start anything."

"I just think you should back off the complaining. We're stuck on a beautiful tropical island, not in the Moab Desert."

"Well, this isn't exactly the Ritz." She flung her hands around, motioning toward the tiki hut. "I don't mind roughing it, but this is a little farfetched." She took a few steps toward the beach. When the water reached her waist, she turned and faced Elliot. "Does anyone even know that we're here?"

"They'll come back soon."

"I'd like to say I believe you, but it's been two weeks now." She moved deeper into the small sea surfs.

He splashed water on her back. "Well, at least you're getting a nice tan. All over."

"Screw the tan."

"Are we fighting?" He tossed the remainder of the spent crab into the cool sea.

"No." She couldn't comprehend why he was so calm about their stranded situation.

"Come here." He took three steps backwards into the surf. His back to the horizon.

"I'm just tired of the smell of the ocean. I'm a city girl— "Her dark eyes popped wide as she scanned the currents.

"Elliot!" she screamed.

The ominous, dark shadow a few feet beneath the clear sea swam toward him.

"You're an unfair fighter–" Elliot said. Then he turned his gaze behind him, seeing the pointed nose bull shark before finishing his sentence.

"–Ryleigh, back up slowly. Don't run. No sudden movements. We're in shallow water, he won't follow us– "Elliot moved backwards as the shark turned toward her.

"Shit!" she said softly. Panic building in the pit of her stomach, pushing its way to her brain.

Elliot stepped in between the shark and Ryleigh, distracting him enough for her to high-knee it toward the shore.

Then everything happened so fast. Elliot swinging his hand with the knife he had pulled from his sheath, which was hardly a match for the shark's mouth full of razor sharp teeth, open and wide.

She saw blood. A lot of blood.

"Elliot!" she screamed, and stopped moving backwards toward the shore's edge.

He was fighting so hard. She thought, *It's going to kill him.* And then she knew it was going to attack her at any second. She felt the panic surge through her bloodstream as she fell in the water and then she tried to stand, but the water felt too deep. She sank down again. The sea smelled like flowers – hibiscus. Sweet hibiscus. She tried to smile in the sweet-smelling water.

Smile, though my heart is aching, Smile even though it's breaking, when there's clouds in the sky, I'll get by...

I'll get by...

He was there at her side, struggling to hold her nose and mouth above water. She kicked and screamed wildly in his arms. What was wrong with her? She was in a few feet of water. She couldn't be drowning.

"Ryleigh, I've got you. Just relax," urged Elliot, trying to sound calm amongst her utter panic.

That's what this is, isn't it? She was still panicked from almost getting attacked by a shark and from almost drowning. She was scared to death. That's had to be why she was fighting Elliot as he was trying to save her. Elliot tried again, louder, "Ryleigh, it's me. It's Elliot! Stop fighting me."

Ryleigh rolled around in the flowers, slapping at the arms wrapping around her. She calmed a little, and when she did, he came back to her and gripped her around the waist and lifted her out of the water – the sea of flowers.

She was drowning again and she swung her arms wildly while he carried her. She was dreaming she was drowning and Elliot was there to save her. But he wasn't there. She was alone on the island, and someone else had found her.

Her first humans had arrived on the island in a flash of arrows and a dash of death. She started sobbing, noisy snot-filled gulping sobs that rang through the hillside.

She didn't know if it was a panic attack, or had the arrow been poisoned? She'd never had a panic attack until recently, but since being stranded, it was a common occurrence. She was feeling really drugged. Her surroundings weren't clear, like a haze, and her body had given up, transpired, and collapsed. She couldn't push forward anymore.

She couldn't see. All was blank, but she dimly felt movement. She seemed to be getting dragged, and dropped down hard.

She assumed that in her own chaotic way she was dreaming, because, somehow, in the poisonous miasma that clouded her head, she realized that this murderer was also saving her.

She tried to speak, in her mind, and her mouth was awfully dry and pasty. No words could form.

THIRTY-SIX

GREG EDERSOM WAS having a meltdown. He had not been in a particularly good mood since he'd seen Ryleigh Lane show up at the courthouse that afternoon.

"How could this happen?" Greg lit a cigarette and took a long drag, forcing the smoke to hang in the air between himself and Ross Palmer. "God damn it."

He paced the garage floor.

"She has an ally," Ross said.

"An ally?"

"Her sister."

"Sister?" His hands were shaking as he took another pull from the cigarette.

"Twin. Identical," Ross said.

Greg forced himself to breathe in and out. He prided himself in knowing people, and especially those that worked for him. He smiled. He had been duped. "Are you sure?"

"The detective mentioned it before–" Ross stopped and bent over, and brushed his hand over his tasseled brown loafer. "–before his random, please-call-for-help, please-don't-kill-me noises came from beneath me."

"What did he say exactly? Are you sure you heard him right? And why would he tell you shit?"

"Well, I had a gun to his head; he'd tell me anything."

"That's not the way I heard it went down. Sam told me that Chandler escaped and snatched your gun, so quit the bullshit. What did he say? Sam said he heard the detective say things like, 'not a chance in hell' and 'over my dead body.' And then your gun went off," Greg said.

"He knew about the impending op, but not too much about the girl alone on the island."

"What did he say before you killed him?"

"It was an accident," Ross said, looking at his shoes.

"What did he say?"

"He said he was going to the island to look for her."

"When?"

"The next day."

"So she is alive still? Hiding on that island?"

"I gathered that."

"Then we'll continue with the explosions. Sooner than planned."

Greg had known there was something off about the Ryleigh girl. A twin sister? He searched his memory. How did he know these twins? He'd be damned if he let her twin testify in Ryleigh's place tomorrow. He'd expose her. He couldn't decide if he wanted the twin dead, too, or in jail. Maybe both. Kill her in prison. He was insanely happy to get rid of both the Lane girls.

One phone call and she won't be testifying tomorrow, Greg thought. He was anxious to leave, and start the earthquake theory. And Caleigh Lane had just earned herself a one-way, non-stop ticket to poisonous snake island.

"What do you want me to do? I can't go near her. Not after the restaurant scene."

"I've got a plan. Is my ride ready?" Greg asked Ross.

"Not yet. We're sweeping the Ferrari for bugs. I found out from the detective that your car was miked."

"Bugs? If the Ferrari is bugged, what about the Benz? Shit, I have some business to take care of. Give me your keys."

"What?" Ross asked, dumbfounded.

"Give me your fucking keys."

"To my van? But – what am I going to drive? I have my tools in there– "

"Quit being such a wuss and stop asking questions. Just shut up and give them to me. You've got a ton of tools here. Sweep the Benz and Ferrari. I want them back clean tomorrow at my place by 8 AM. I have a few stops to make and can't do it in my wheels."

Ross looked like he was about to protest again, but Greg grabbed the car keys from Ross's clenched hands.

Greg walked across the concrete driveway with the weeds popping through the cracked cement. He jumped into the driver's side of the van and slammed the door. It smelt like a French fry grease machine, a gerbil's cage, and cleaning fluid.

The floorboards were filled with piles of trash, ketchup packets, clumps of napkins, and CDs.

Greg put the van in gear and moved down the driveway. "I think I know how to kill two birds with one stone."

He picked up the phone and dialed. "Can you kidnap the Ryleigh girl? Yep. Immediately"

He hung up the phone. Caleigh belonged with her sister, where both girls would die alone on the island.

THIRTY-SEVEN

THE NIGHT AIR in the Chicago suburb was still. Caleigh stood on the large porch, away from the abominable city and away from the evilly disposed Dexco thugs. "Sounds like a plan. Be safe, Elliot."

"I will. Promise. You're in good hands with Dice. Get some sleep; you have an early morning."

Caleigh hugged him goodbye, but it was different than the previous hugs she'd given him, with a genuine concern for her, a special family bond. She forced a smile. "Go rescue our girl before she goes crazy from being alone."

He paused outside on the steps and they gave each other one last look.

She stood on the porch and caught her reflection in the living room window. She looked tired, and yet at the same time refreshed. It occurred to her that she had a very important day tomorrow, and she would be holed up with Dice for the night, while Elliot flew halfway across the globe to some unknown island.

She heard the heavy iron gates in the garden shut for the night, and those sounds instantly sank her into silence. Concerned for her twin, she felt a sinking sensation in the pit of her stomach, nerves.

Dice was standing by the window, staring out, and she wasn't sure he had heard her come in. She wanted him to tell her about the conversation he'd had with Elliot earlier that night, but she didn't think he was going to talk. At times, she wondered if it was better not to know the truth, until after her testimony.

The fireplace glow lit the room and, for an instant, it reminded Caleigh of her little yellow house on Central. A safe house. A place she'd no longer felt at home in, since the accident. She walked over to Dice and covered his hand with hers. He turned toward her and his eyes were alert with apprehension, given what he was there to do, to be her bodyguard.

Dice was a handsome man, tough but with warm eyes. He leaned forward, resting one arm on her shoulder. "Are you okay?"

"I'm fine, just tired. There's so much I want to know; I need to know. But I'm afraid to find out more before my testimony. I'll be the first to say, it could sway my answers if I knew."

"That's why we can't tell you, Caleigh. You don't need to worry, and you need to trust in us."

"I do. But ever since I got that call a month ago on my voicemail..."

"The call?"

"Yes. Didn't Elliot tell you? It was a random voicemail from Ryleigh. It came from her cell phone. She yelled that she needed help. Then she yelled, 'Stop, Elliot.' And the phone went dead."

"What are you saying? Did you ask Elliot?"

"I did, and he said Ryleigh had found her phone hidden in the sand the first day they were left behind on the island. She was able to power it on and she called me."

She called me.

"Why did she yell for help?" Dice asked.

"Elliot said that a feral hog had attacked her and she'd jumped into the sea. After that, her phone died."

"And you don't believe Elliot?"

"I believe him, I guess." She was afraid to say much more.

"There's something else you're not saying?" Dice said, lifting his eyebrows.

She wanted to tell him that anyone with only an ounce of courage could not have agreed to stay stranded alone on an island. That her sister had to have fallen totally in love and in trust with Elliot to agree to the plan. Or maybe she was being held there against her will. Maybe Ryleigh had her own agenda. But she didn't bring it up, not to Elliot's best friend. So she shook her head.

"All right then, let's finish the testimony run-through."

She yawned.

Dice checked his watch. "It is getting late. Your testimony is in the morning. Do you want to get a good night's sleep and we'll do a run-through at breakfast?"

His voice was low, soft. Dice stood staring at her. She stared back. Just looking at him made her feel calmer, safe.

When she didn't answer, he moved in closer and touched his lips to hers. The pressure was soft and the kiss warm. Caleigh responded and Dice tasted like her deepest craving fulfilled, and smelled like fire. She placed her hand around his neck, and he kissed her harder.

He felt strong and safe. But Caleigh knew they had to stop. *Stop*, she told herself. But she pushed in closer to him.

It was Dice who pulled back. Just enough to look into her eyes.

"Well, sleepy girl, you need to get to bed." His wonderful eyes pleaded with her, but he never let go of her waist.

She felt a stab of guilt when he wouldn't let go. But she knew she had to call it a night.

"Okay, I'm going to bed," she said, frowning.

"Or you can sleep on the couch for a while if you want. I'll keep you company, but I can't sleep."

"You have to sleep. Won't you stay in the guest room?" That was when she felt his arms loosen from her.

"I may later. But I want to stay close to the downstairs doors and windows."

"Oh," she said, narrowing her eyes.

"You'll be safe here on the couch or upstairs, Caleigh." Dice slipped out of her arms.

"Well then, it's good night." She left his side and paused at the stair landing. "Will you wake me? I don't trust my cell alarm because I'm really exhausted." His sweet kiss still lingered on her mouth and she felt happy to carry it to bed with her.

"Yes. No problem. How about o' seven hundred?"

"Perfect."

"Good night, Caleigh."

"Good night, Dice, "she said, trying out the sweet words she could get used to saying.

THIRTY-EIGHT

GREG DETOURED around the Chicago streets heading towards Lake Michigan before returning to his office. He needed time to think.

The Lane girls were up to something, so he decided to advance his plans.

His hands fumbled with his cell phone, a little shaky from too much coffee and his bad news.

"How soon can we start the explosions in the islands?" Greg squinted at his reflection in the rearview mirror; he looked frayed around the edges. He worked long hours, and plus now he had to deal with the trial and a shitload of other surprises waiting in the islands. At least the trial would be off his plate, with their star witness, or should he say star *witnesses*, having done a disappearing act. He hoped Caleigh now on her way to being reunited with her sister.

"Yeah, I'm here. Make sure that they start with the island left of Keg Key. Then blow Keg Key."

He noticed a police cruiser pull onto the street, five cars behind him, and turned off a side street. Lake Michigan was visible at the end of the street. His mind was on the islands and the surprises they held.

"Yep, blow the fucker up, concentrating on the caves. My team will be there the following day to explore the excavation."

The van stopped at a red light. Suddenly, the car behind his hit the rear bumper of the van and started pushing it through the intersection.

"What the fuck? I gotta go! Call Ross and tell him to meet me at the office with my Benz."

Greg wanted to ditch the van; the smell inside had gotten noticeably worst since he'd left the suburbs and driven to the city, and now some lunatic was pushing the van forward toward the traffic.

Greg looked in the mirror and saw a man in a leather jacket behind the wheel. He heard sounds of crashing and scraping metal as the van was pushed by the tailing car.

He held the brake pedal to the floor, and a cloud of smoke engulfed his car from the burning tires as the other car spun on the street, pushing the van through the intersection.

Holding the brake, he was pushed into the intersection, barely avoiding a speeding car.

Greg looked to the right and saw a break in the traffic, and floored the accelerator. He passed a few cars, but the car pushing his bumper came fishtailing through the intersection, gaining on him.

His heart raced when he saw the car on his tail. He smelled burnt rubber as he two-wheeled the van over a curb, just avoiding crashing into several parked cars. The car followed directly behind him.

Greg intentionally drove toward the side street he had seen the police cruiser go down. He had the gas pedal floored, and almost lost control as he sped past a cop car going in the opposite direction.

The police car did a U-turn and approached the van with flashing lights and a siren blasting. The car trailing him suddenly passed the van and the driver flipped him the finger.

Greg pulled the van to the curb and leaned his head out the rolled-down window as the officer approached.

"I'm glad to see you, officer. Did you see that car try and push me through the intersection?"

He shook his head. "Your driver's license please."

Greg reached into his back pocket and retrieved his wallet. Relieved that, when the officer called in his license, he would get treated with respect, like he always did in his city.

"You were driving forty miles an hour over the speed limit."

"I was being followed."

The officer looked up and down the street.

"Your van plates are expired, and you're dragging a rope."

"Did you hear me? I was being pushed into oncoming traffic, by some lunatic. I had to speed away from him. This isn't my van, either."

Greg reached for the car door and started to step out.

"Wait here. And stay in the car."

Greg sat in the dark car as the police officer called in his license.

While he was in his squad car, two other police vehicles showed up.

"Shit. This isn't good."

Three police officers joined the lone officer that had his license.

"Mr. Edersom?"

"Yes, that's me. CEO of Dexco. This isn't my van."

"Well, we need to bring you in."

"What?"

"There's a warrant out for the owner of this vehicle, and maybe you can help us clear up a few things."

"I'm late. Can someone drive me to my office? Then I'll come downtown later. Clear this all up." He flashed his politician smile.

"Do you mind if we look in the van?"

"Sure. Go ahead. It belongs to a mechanic. Can you hurry it up? I've got to get to my office."

"We'll only be a few minutes, Mr. Edersom."

It was quiet in the street, almost eerie, when the four officers, and Greg opened the van's back doors.

The van floor was covered with fast food bags, and tools and toolboxes. Mostly mechanics' metal toolkits.

Greg had started to turn away and walk back to the driver's side of the van when something on the carpet caught his attention. It caught one of the policeman's attention, too.

Bending over into the van, the first policeman that had pulled him over reached for an object, but he gasped and withdrew his hand before touching it.

It was a hunting knife, with a six to eight-inch blade covered in what appeared to be blood.

Four flashlights pointed at the van's floor. One of the larger metal toolboxes was slightly opened. The gray toolbox was approximately 4 feet long, and the lid was slightly ajar.

One beam of light trailed to it, and the policeman nodded to another.

"Mr. Edersom, step back. Put your hands behind you."

Crap. Now what had Ross done?

"This isn't my vehicle," Greg said as one of the officers cuffed his hands behind his back.

"Oh, shit. We've got a body!"

Greg turned around to face the back of the van. He couldn't believe his eyes. Inside the large metal toolbox was a mixture of body parts. Limbs cut from the torso and a head detached from the body, all neatly jammed inside the toolbox.

The street was quiet, and the only sound Greg heard was a car horn in the distance, and his own vomit splattering the pavement in front of him.

THIRTY-NINE

SOMETHING WOKE CALEIGH.

She tried to recall the noise. A chill ran up her back. It was the gate.

Someone or something had clanged the gate.

She tried to fall back asleep, but her racing mind kept her up. Was it Josh and Denny changing shifts? Was it Dice leaving? *But he said he would be here when I woke up.*

Before she could fall asleep again, she felt a warm hand cover her mouth. Her eyes went wide until she recognized Dice kneeling alongside the bed. He touched a finger to his lips and beckoned for her to follow him.

She slid out of the bed, her heart bouncing around.

They walked to the end of the hallway and turned a corner. Dice pulled her into the guest bedroom and then into a walk-in closet.

"What is it?" she whispered.

"Someone's here." Dice had leaned in and whispered back.

Caleigh was physically shaking. She was barefoot, and she curled her toes to protect them from the chill that ran through the dark closet.

Dice narrowed his eyes. "You have to stay in here until I investigate. Lie flat under the clothes to keep warm."

It was then that Caleigh realized there were rows of clothing hanging in the guest room closet. Which she would have found peculiar in an unoccupied safe house, but the thought was not a concern at the moment.

"When will you be back? Can I go with you?" A fear and panic came over Caleigh.

"I won't be long. Lay down and I'll be back in five minutes."

Her legs turned to taffy, and she hoped he hadn't noticed. She thought about the infrared listening devices, and that gave her some sense of comfort now, knowing that they were being monitored beyond the iron gate, but it didn't stop her trembling legs.

Caleigh wanted to say something to Dice, but the moment passed. She gave him a nod with her eyes, squeezed his hand, and fell to the floor. Shivering, Caleigh felt her lips tremble for a short moment as she watched him leave. She would wait five minutes. She was on her own for now.

She was in full-body lockdown, flat against the floor, listening. Besides her heart thumpty-thump racing, there were no other sounds, except a clock in the bedroom ticking.

It had been at least two minutes. Two numbing minutes of insane waiting. She needed to find out what was going on firsthand. Maybe Dice needed her. But she decided to wait three more minutes.

She jumped when she felt a large hand grab her goose-pimpled leg and yank her out of the closet. She clawed at the carpeted floor, grabbing at the low-hanging row of jeans, but her assailant was strong.

"Let's go, missy," a ski-masked man said while throwing a dark pillowcase over her head as she stood up.

Caleigh started to scream, but stopped when he smacked the side of her head.

Jesus God, Help Me.

FORTY

A SINGLE THOUGHT raced through Caleigh's head. *Where is Dice?*

She had been led downstairs, first stopping at the bedroom, where her masked man told her to dress warmly. She had taken that as a good sign, because if he'd been going to dump her dead body into Lake Michigan, warm clothes wouldn't have mattered. She had thrown on a pair of jeans, socks, suede boots, and a sweatshirt.

She wanted to ask questions, but was afraid to irritate him. *Don't overthink this, Caleigh. Just ask him.*

"Where's Dice?" she asked through her pillowcase hood.

No answer.

"And Denny?"

Silence.

"What about Josh?" She trotted alongside him, her eyes trying to make out his fuzzy shadow of an outline through the thin pillowcase.

"They're shit out of luck. Just like you if you don't follow my directions."

Caleigh's insides ached. *Dice. His team? What happened to all of them?*

"Here," he said, handing her a round, hard object. "Put this on."

"Remember, I can't see. Take this hood off my head and I'll– "

She felt him grasp the object from her hand. He crammed a helmet onto her head, then lifted the pillowcase halfway up, tucking it over her ears. She still couldn't see, but she could breathe better.

"Are we going skydiving? Or skiing?" She acted brave on the outside, but inside she was a mess.

He grabbed her arm, and she was prepared to be tied up, but instead he jammed it into a large, leathery sleeve. First her left, then her right.

He led her outside and pulled her down the path toward the gate. The cold air prickled at her mouth and throat. She waited for Elliot's team to jump out, but with each step, she had a sinking feeling in her stomach that they weren't watching the two red outlines of humans bleeding body heat as they crossed the back of the safe house.

She was having trouble thinking. What would be her next move? Was he going to hurt her, or worse, kill her?

Before she had left Italy, thoughts like this had never occurred to her. She felt confident of her long lifespan, but since coming to Chicago and helping Elliot and Ryleigh, she had worried daily about her life.

He pulled her to the left. The path leading to the brick building would be to the right. *Did he disarm the infrared? Did he hurt and disarm my bodyguards? Or worse?*

They walked along the rough path. Caleigh stumbled on a rock and fell to her knees.

"Can you take this off my eyes? I can't see your face. You have a mask on." Or maybe he had taken it off.

"Shut up."

She had to walk fast because he was pulling her hard and forcefully down a path. It didn't take long for her body to warm up from wearing the leather coat and heavy helmet, and from the exertion of being pulled this way and that.

They reached a clearing. Maybe a street. She listened for city street noises; the rustle of joggers' feet, newspapers being delivered, cars rolling by, or trash being removed. She heard nothing distinct, not even chirping birds.

It had been around three o'clock when Dice awoke Caleigh. *Not too many people out strolling this time of the morning,* she thought.

She waited to be tossed in the back of a van.

He started a motorcycle. It sounded like something detonating.

PAMELA LAUX MOLL

FORTY-ONE

CALEIGH STOOD quivering, her voice a hoarse, frightened whisper. "Where are we going?"

"You're going to get on and hang on to me like you know me. Don't try anything or they will hunt you down and–"

"I can't see."

It was then that he pulled the pillowcase up, exposing her eyes, but still tucking it into the helmet. *What was the point of not removing it?* The pillowcase reminded Caleigh of trick-or-treating. She and Ryleigh had used pillowcases off their beds on Halloween to hold their candy and goodies.

What kidnappers used linens in their capers? And drove motorcycles with their victim on the back in plain sight? Either a stupid one or a confident one.

Her eyes, tearing from the dust of the blindfold, tried focusing in the dark. She saw the black shiny motorcycle in front of her. She turned toward the ski-masked man, but he had replaced the mask with a full-face helmet, making his head almost invisible at night. She couldn't even see his beady, dark brown eyes, like she'd been able to through the mask holes, before he'd covered her head. He was about six-foot-tall, wore all black, and looked geared up for a burglary or an assassination of a team of special agents. His belt held an empty holster, spare magazines, a Taser, and two cell phones. The whole-nine-yards belt was ready for an attack. Obviously, this man hadn't come by for hot chocolate and idle chit-chat.

"Get on."

That was when Caleigh saw the gun. A small caliber pistol in his right hand. And something else. Blood.

His hand had dried blood on the knuckles. *Whose blood?*

A second later, she felt the gun sticking under her armpit. "I'm not going to ask you again. Jump on. And don't try anything stupid."

"Stupid. This whole thing is stupid. Can we just talk about tomorrow's– "

"Cut the bullshit." He dug the revolver into her ribs.

Caleigh jumped on the back of the bike, held the grab rail, and pressed up against the backrest. He flipped something down on her helmet and everything went dark again. She couldn't see in her peripheral vision, making it difficult to hold on, and the image of him in front of her was a blur.

His voice sounded in her helmet. "Can you hear me?"

"Yes. But I can't see you. I guess that's the idea. How am I going to hang on?"

"Shut the fuck up. Or I won't deliver you."

Deliver her? Where?

"Hang on to the leather seat, and my waist if needed. "She felt him strap a belt across her waist, and then another strap on her wrist which was fastened to his belt.

"This is cozy, "she said as an unsettling fear rattled through her. This moment felt like her last chance to get away. She needed to stall. Caleigh swiveled around in the seat.

"I'm warning you. Don't try nothing fancy. I want you to be a sack of potatoes strapped to the back seat. If not, I will be delivering a corpse to them."

"This sack of potatoes is human, and I want to know where Dice is at."

"I warned you to shut up."

She couldn't let him drive away from the safe house compound. The weight of Dice's life, the trial, and Dexco's murderous actions kept Caleigh talking. She had to stall and risk being heard by anyone.

"You don't want me to fall off and make mashed potatoes, do you? Sounds like they want me alive."

"Sarcastic bitch. This will quiet you."

A long object poked against her stomach, and she felt a jolt and a wall of pain shoot through her entire body. Her body tensed up and she experienced a pulsating sensation to her muscles that lasted about five seconds.

Strapped onto the bike, she fell forward against the motorcycle driver's back.

She barely heard the whisper in the helmet. "Now do I have your attention?"

Her abs were a sheet of pain. She moaned but withheld the scream in her throat.

"Don't make a sound or you'll have a bullet hole in that tiny waist!"

Her mind came up with a million reasons to get the energy to break away, but her body came up with only one reason to just lie there against him, like two lovers out for an early morning cruise, but it was one good reason. What if the Taser caused heart failure? Or unconsciousness? Then she wouldn't be able to pay attention to where they were taking her.

Caleigh wiggled and felt she was suffocating.

The voice inside her helmet spoke to her, "Do you want another round? I've been charging it all night. I've got plenty of juice."

Strength was coming back to Caleigh, but she knew she couldn't take another shot from the gun.

But stalling might help. What if there was someone nearby watching? Or Dice and his team were closing in? Was it worth another shot from the Taser leads?

She searched her photographic memory for articles about people getting Tased. She remembered a hardened felony being Tased. He'd fallen down and cried like a baby after being hit with the police Taser. He had been taken into custody without anyone getting hurt, and he'd had no physical fall-out.

Caleigh balled her free hand into a fist. "You couldn't handle a little woman like me, all by yourself," she said. Her voice sounded funny-hollow and slurred. She swung her fist at his side, catching some of her knuckles under the hard belt.

"You bitch."

This time, it was like a wall of buzzing. It lasted longer. Maybe ten seconds. Ten seconds of a lethal dose of pain, causing her body to twitch, jerk, and fall forward. She bit her tongue and tasted blood in her mouth.

She forced her body to go limp, so he would think she had blacked out. She prayed that she would drop into unconsciousness. But she didn't.

The cushioned backseat was oversized, where Caleigh was slumped, strapped in and with her arms wrapped around the driver, giving her limp body no choice but to lean against him. The wheels spun in the quiet street's gravel. The driver pulled his belt tighter, forcing her tightly against him. And they rode into the dark night.

FORTY-TWO
THE LAGOON

RYLEIGH DID NOT know how she had found the strength to move, let alone run, but she did. Plunging through the field of dense foliage, expecting at any moment to feel the sting of an arrow, or the grip of an unfriendly hand clasp around her. The mangroves gave way all of a sudden, she half-crawled, half scampered through the path of thick bushes until the earth dipped steeply and abruptly.

She was on the bank of the lagoon. Could she swim to the cave? She had no choice but to try to cross under the waterfall. Drowning was not the worst fate she decided.

She slid down the bank, and waded a few feet into the water. All her energy focused on keeping her head above water and paddling with her arms, dragging her injured foot behind her.

How much torment, both physical and mental, could she endure?

FORTY-THREE

WHEN RYLEIGH AWOKE, the last few days seemed to her a blur. She remembered almost drowning, but now she found herself lying flat on her back inside the cave. How did she get there? She couldn't remember swimming.

Although the darkness impaired her sight, she could still make out a faint glow, and the familiar smells from the insides of an island cave. *Which cave? The lagoon? Under the waterfall?*

She sat up and felt the cool, damp air that smelt of rat or bat urine. Or another human? Which was a good sign, because that meant she was near an entrance or exit. Animals don't live long inside dark caves, and usually just go there for shelter. With her swollen ankle, she prayed the opening was nearby.

Her eyes, ears, and nose searched the surrounding blackness for any signs of another human. She recalled being dragged in in her semi-conscious state. *Who brought me here? And why?*

Ryleigh reached into Elliot's sheath, wrapped around her shrinking waist, and discovered her knife was still there. *Thank God.*

But the maps?

They were both gone! The one that she'd had and the one she'd found on the dead man, both missing.

She tried to stand and a wall of pain raced up her leg. Ryleigh tested the dirt floor with her good leg, and finding it stable, moved forward. She shuffled her feet in the dark, using the damp low walls to cling to for guidance.

"Hello," she said, and her words echoed back to her after a nano-second. "Is anyone there? Did you bring me here?"

Ryleigh limped toward the soft light that fluttered in the corner of the low walled cave. She felt a movement in the air, from either a bat, snake, an animal, Captain Trevor's murderer, or...

"Hello?" she whispered.

The air moved again. Was someone there watching her?

Painfully, she continued to place one foot in front of the other.

How long did I lie there? I didn't know. To me, it seemed like a day or so.

A low rustle came from behind her. She swirled around and a rush of lightheadedness overcame her.

Her vision evaporated in blackness for a few seconds. Ryleigh sank with her back against the cave wall and held her spinning head in her hands.

"Damn it. Get a grip." She tried standing again slowly. Her fear of the dark cave diminishing as her anger at the stolen maps rose.

Something flashed low in the wall again.

She had no idea about the cave's filigree of channels and caverns. Was she deep in the cave? Watching for the faint flash of light coming from a place near the cave's floor, she heard the scuffle of rodents' feet and the strong smell of their excrement.

This led her to blindly follow their sound toward a small opening in the wall close to the cave floor. "This is where the light flashed from," she said, kneeling.

The thought of her climbing through a dark tunnel in a cave gave her chills. "I can't even stand the confined space of going through a car wash."

She remembered hearing how tortoises had sought cave shelters to get relief from the hot tropical sun. The faint flash of light popped again.

"Oh darn. I'm going to have to try it." She had never experienced such a sickening claustrophobic panic, which perhaps had numbed her fear temporarily.

Plopping down on her tummy, she attempted a superman crawl through the constrictive tunnel. The only way she could fit through the tunnel was by holding one arm tightly against her body and extending the other overhead, like the Man of Steel in flight. After several feet of wiggling through the horizontal chute, she could feel herself wading through rat excrement. Had her torso been slightly fatter, she would not have even fit in the narrow chute. The tunnel floor was greasy slick with dung and moss. She forced her arm, her head, and her shoulders down into the blackness, pushing toward the flash of light.

She dug her sore foot into the tunnel's grimy floor and used her outstretched hand, holding the knife, to bulldoze the path.

"This passageway can't be the way I got here. Logically then, it won't be the way out," she murmured between holding her breath.

Between the sheer amount of dung in the cave's tunnel, breathing back in her own carbon dioxide, heat, humidity, and who knew what other contaminants were in the air, it all made her start to hyperventilate. Rapidly taking deep, quick breaths, she tried to calm her anxiety attack.

"Back out. Back out. Go. Go. I have to get out," she gasped, wiggling backwards.

Huffing and inching, she crawfished her way out of the tubular tunnel. The tiny flashes of light sparked and disappeared as she reentered the large cavern. The dark, huge catacomb of caves was safer than the tiny, narrow pocket.

She peered into the darkness, her chin quivering, and several silent tears slid down her cheek. Relieved, she wasn't panicky anymore, but afraid, yes. She had almost lost it in the tunnel. She covered her mouth and fought back nausea.

As Ryleigh leaned against the cave wall, she sat straighter, suddenly paying attention to a slight shadowy movement in the dark air.

Her eyes attempting to pierce the shadows, she thought she could make out a shadow further into the cave behind her. Squinting, she tried to focus. Slowly, she withdrew the large knife from the sheath again.

"Who's there?"

After a couple of seconds, she yelled, "Is somebody there?"

An echo. Then silence.

She spoke in a normal voice that sounded inexplicably loud in the cave. "Did you take the maps?"

Now frozen by anger rather than fear, she aimed her knife into the darkness. "I can help you. I know the location of the treasures. If you can help me out of here. And I'm hungry and thirsty. Did you come here through the tunnel?"

Her dehydration was at the highest it had been. She knew it was partially from her diabetes, but also from the loss of blood.

"Did you carry me here? What cave are we in?" She stepped forward, and the aches in her ankle and body settled into a dull, throbbing pain.

A moment passed, Ryleigh still leaning against the short cave wall, her body hunched over like an old lady's.

She shuffled toward the faint light, which seemed miles from where she stood. She stepped cautiously forward, edging in the dark to the faint dime-size light, groping with stretched-out arms, military style, left, right, left, right, to the sides.

As she shuffled along gingerly with her feet, she heard a slight, sandpapery scraping noise. "Hello?"

If there was another person lurking near her, she couldn't see or smell them. The only smells were of the black mold on the damp cave walls, bat dung, and her own body odor mixing in with her fading sunscreen.

She kicked herself now for not bringing a flashlight. Even though the small light would barely have cut the darkness, she could at least have seen in front of herself by a few feet.

"I'm moving forward. I have a weapon, and if there's someone in here with me that means to harm me, I will use it."

She assumed whoever had brought her there didn't have a gun. But a gun or a bow and arrow were useless here, in the dark cave. They were strong, though – at least strong enough to carry or drag her to the cave.

Ryleigh was strong, too. She swam laps in the sea every day, and walked the beach and hiked the island. Yes, she was skinny, but under her thin exterior was a lot of muscle. Women back home in Chicago would die for her body, and her tan.

For a fleeting second, Ryleigh felt lonely, and not the kind of loneliness that had anything to do with her being stranded alone on an island, or with being held hostage in a cave, but the sad feeling of the lack of another human interaction.

Her eyes blurred moist. "Elliot," she whispered. She shuffled a few more feet forward, not caring if she ran into a human murderer, a rat, a snake, or anything.

"It's not like it matters, anyway." But it did matter. She needed to get out of the cave alive, return to her camp, and feed Ebba, and wait for Elliot.

She stuck her knife back into her makeshift sheath. Her hands were trembling anyway. And the chances of her tripping and landing on her own knife were greater than her stabbing an aberration in the dark.

She expected to be attacked when she put her knife away, but nothing happened.

The pain in her swollen foot crept up her leg with each baby step she took. She moved toward the tiny dot of light, fighting back the scream that was building in her mouth.

Tired and confused, she leaned against the wall, and slid down into a crouching position. Any muscles that she had were flinching from agony.

She shut her eyes and was overwhelmed by the dark.

FORTY-FOUR

RYLEIGH WOKE UP to a drenching rain. It fell from the dark sky and ran down her chin. How had she gotten out of the cave?

With her eyes wide open, she realized the blackness she saw in front of her and all around her was the inside of the cave. The water on her face was her sweat. Her skimpy clothes were still damp.

Of course, she had passed out again. Sleep-deprived for the last few days. How long had she been by the lagoon now and how long had she been in this cave? She had visions of drowning and being held underwater.

She needed to walk toward the light, to move methodically forward. Standing still wasn't an option.

She took baby steps. Stopping every few feet to kneel down, and to feel around the ground. At this stoppage, she came across a smooth, long object, a blunt stick of some type. And then she felt more sticks with points neatly placed in a row. It felt like the crushed remains of a large animal. The rib cage.

Fanning her hands on the floor, she felt more of the smooth objects. She ran her hand along the skull. It wasn't an animal, she realized. It was a human.

My God, she thought, scrambling backwards until she bumped into the wall. Who had died here?

Her chest struggled to take in the cave's musty air. Calm breathing. Relax. Deep breaths, she told herself.

After feeling the remains of another human in the cave, Ryleigh knew this, that she wasn't going to be the cave's next victim. She wasn't sure how she'd make it out, but what she did know, is that she wasn't going to die boxed in by rock and dirt walls, and that she'd do whatever it took to escape. No way was she dying in this dark, damp cave. No damn way.

On wobbly legs, she stood and journeyed forward, around the human remains.

Imagining the typology of the cave, she knew they formed as rainwater or the surrounding lagoon dissolved the surrounding rocks, creating a special cavernous structure underground.

Feeling damp tree roots protruding from the cave's soft stony walls gave her hope that beyond the thin interior layer was a way out. As she felt around the caves, the walls seemed to widen, and the cooler air gave her the feeling she had entered a large alcove. Her blind touching and tiny steps in all directions made her deduce that the small space was parlor sized. That was progress. Earlier, she'd felt she was trapped in a narrow closet.

I'll never go close to the caves again without carrying a flashlight. Why hadn't she brought one with her? But of course, it was bright daylight when she had left. She would never even go for a walk without bringing them with her.

She heard faint squeaks of sleeping bats in the cave's hollow corridors. This sound she knew, and it told her it was daylight outside. But for how long? This felt reassuring, since at dusk the colony of bats would leave the cave to hunt insects. At minimum, maybe she could follow them out.

At this moment, she wished she'd paid more attention in science class. Would the bats sleep in their roost closer to an entrance? Or fly a great distance in the caves to exit? She had no clue. However, it made more sense to Ryleigh that the bats would set up their nests farther away from the entrance. Away from wind, predators, and any ambient light.

Listening again for the bat sounds, she felt they seemed to have the qualities of a ventriloquist. Their faint squeaks appeared to come first from the left and then the right, making it very hard for her to follow.

Her visibility was nothing. When she closed her eyes, occasionally small purple bony streaks of light burst in front of her eyelids, but she knew she was tired and that these were images pounding out of her brain. Like dreams bouncing in front of her closed eyes.

As she traveled deeper, she realized the squeaky sounds grew fainter, so she kept moving forward, her hands searching braille on the porous walls. The stench of rat or bat dung, or both, made her hold her breath on and off.

The cave floors and walls felt covered with the hardened feces from the bats and rats. Flying rodents in the air, and squirming rodents on the floor. Her lucky day.

Keg Key was full of flying insects, colorful birds, and at night, the bats. The forests and caves seemed to be home to some of the largest bats she'd ever seen. Elliot had come across a dead one last month. It looked like a flying fox. She often wondered how many of the species found on the island, like Ebba, had reached this far-stretching section of the South Pacific atoll.

Ryleigh took a few tentative steps and collided with a hard surface about two feet tall. She was bent over the surface of something oval-shaped. She ran her hand over the surface.

"Ouch," she yelled out as she felt a sharp sting in her finger. At first, she thought it to be a centipede bite. But the pain was familiar. She rubbed her fingers against the source of the pain, and recognized it. A splinter.

She scratched, until she could grasp the tiny wood splinter from under her skin and pull it from her finger. She scooted her wounded leg slightly to the right of the hard object. Once again, she ran into the hard surface and fell over.

She had an "Eureka!" moment in silence. She wanted to shout out that she had found it, but she wasn't sure yet if she was still alone in the cave.

FORTY-FIVE

RYLEIGH BENT IN HALF at the waist ran her hand cautiously over the second hard surface. Smelling and feeling it.

She chuckled. "I think I've got myself bent over a barrel." She laughed again, harder. Not caring about anyone or anything around her. Her hysterical laughs filled and echoed throughout the cave. Her inside ached from laughing and tears filled her eyes.

The kegs!

She couldn't see them, but for the first time in a long time, her heart had begun to pump with crazy hope. Her fingers twitched and yearned to unfold the map. The hairs on her skin stood up.

When she tripped again and pushed against another hollow drum shape, she whispered to herself, "Finders keepers." *And to the victors in life go life's spoils.*

She had been right all along. The caves held kegs or barrels. The treasure map had unidentified marks on it and, based on her research and assumptions, it was the barrels that marked the spot. This was huge. And important. Important to Ryleigh. An over-obsession-type of importance. Didn't these kegs or barrels mean something?

She leaned over a barrel and shook it. It wobbled and fell over and collapsed, bringing her down with it. She heard cracking sounds, like decayed wood snapping. She smelt vinegar and ammonia and something else. What was that?

Damn. Why hadn't she brought a flashlight? She sat still on the hard, dusty floor, trying to see around her. The small speck of light down the dark cave tunnel had never looked so inviting. She moved between the two barrels and used the one still intact to gently pull herself up. Now her thoughts went to how she had gotten into the cave with the barrels.

She couldn't see inside the cave, but she was certain it was filled with the rotting barrels. That was the smell that she had awoken to.

But who had brought her here? How had she ended up in this cave? Why would they shoot at her, steal her maps, and leave her for dead, in the cave that she had been searching for? Searching for a long time.

She felt a spider web across her face.

X marks the spot with a dot, dot, dot and a dash, dash, dash, and a big question mark. Spiders crawling up your back, now they're crawling down your back. Feel a cool breeze and a squeeze, now you have the chills...

In truth, while she had been looking really hard at this, someone else was, too. "Who's here with me?" She yelled, "Hello!"

Hello, hello, hello... echoed off the cave walls. Who else was aware of these kegs?

Then she felt it. Very slowly, she reached for her knife and pulled it out and held it firmly in front of her. Someone was there. She could feel their presence in the cave. Was it an evil or good presence?

She knew that as soon as they made a sound or a move to hurt her, she could be all over them with the knife.

10 knives in your back. Let the blood flow down. Crack an egg on your head. Let the yolk flow down.

She listened and stood firmly between the two barrels. Her nerves of steel were now a thin thread of rubber, bouncing around back and forth, ready for anything. She stayed still and now avoided the dim light at the end of the cave, because that would ruin whatever dark cave vision she was developing. She stared into the dark, damp cavern. Her foot throbbing, her feet so cold she curled her toes to keep them warm.

She knew her foot was bleeding again, but she felt that was good, as it would flush the wound of infection. She quietly tightened the bandana wrapped around her foot.

A few minutes passed, and she wondered if her intuition of another person being in the cave was accurate.

Ryleigh slowly knelt and felt around on the cave floor until she came upon a small rock. She picked it up and waited. Another few minutes passed, and when Ryleigh was almost sure she was alone, she gently tossed the rock forward toward the dim light at the cave tunnel, throwing it so it would go three to four feet in front of her.

The rock hit a surface, maybe another keg, and bounced off it and fell to the cave floor.

She saw a glint in the dark. Was it a glint from a knife? A person's eyes? She tried to make it out, but she couldn't. She waited, holding her breath. The more she tried to make out the glint in the dark, the more she couldn't figure it out.

It was hard for her to not talk. She assumed the person that had brought her to the cave didn't want to kill her. But what if she was wrong? She moved away from the two barrels. Slowly and quietly moving toward the light.

She felt the air move to her left and she charged the movement with her body and knife. She collided with another keg and her knife scraped the cave's rock floor.

She couldn't stand the silence and the unknowing.

The makeshift bandages on her foot stung with pins and needles as both feet stepped on glass. Shards of tiny splinters of glass now penetrated the soles of her feet.

Ryleigh had been so lost in introspection that it took a moment to focus her attention away from her fear to what she felt piercing the soles of her feet. *What could this be now?*

Her good foot was now peppered with shards of glass. Leaning over the barrel, she pulled the pieces of glass from her blood-caked feet. Focus. Stay focused. Pulling the pieces of glass from her feet, she slowly stood up. Feeling dizzy, but fortuitous, she held on to the barrel for support.

Could this nightmare get any worse?

And it did.

She heard the familiar thump, thump, thump of a helicopter overhead.

Ryleigh had waited for this day to come, and now Elliot was here on the island, but she wasn't anywhere to be rescued.

FORTY-SIX

OVER THE SOUTH PACIFIC waters, an hour had easily passed since they had left the ship. Through a cloudless sky, dozens of islands began to appear. To Elliot, it was not just breathtaking as seen from this vantage point, but as the helicopter began to approach Keg Key, the island increasingly grew in size, and so did the lump in his throat.

The chopper flew over an area situated directly beneath them, where many islets were exposed, huddled closely together. Brush Island. Snake Island.

Out of those islets, which became clearer by the second, one became bigger than the rest. A secluded excursion island held with much secrecy from any other visitors to the area, small but effective, easy on the eye, and located about twenty miles from the cruise ship port.

It seemed like only days ago that he and Ryleigh had ventured away from the excursion group to this isolated island, Keg Key.

It took all of Elliot Finn's restraint to keep himself from jumping out of the chopper as the familiar paths and beaches flew by under him. He was back on Keg Key and minutes away from seeing Ryleigh. They flew over the now broken apart pile of rocks that at one time, many weeks ago, had spelled "HELP" and "SOS".

"Stay over the woods another hundred yards, and then you'll see a clearing that opens onto the beach!" Elliot yelled. He had removed his headphones, preparing for his drop onto Keg Key beach. Hovering over the familiar shores of Keg Key, Elliot could easily make out the tiki hut. His heart sank when there were no immediate signs of Ryleigh.

When the chopper was high over the tiki beach, it hovered.

"Look there," the pilot of the copter pointed. "We've got a body."

Elliot's eyes adjusted over the glare of the sea. An outline of a body floated face down, arms spread wide, head underwater. His heart raced as the chopper neared. For a few seconds, thoughts of Ryleigh giving up and drowning herself flew by in his head. Why was that his first thought?

As the chopper dipped lower, Elliot used binoculars, beneath his flight helmet, to search the sea.

He searched over the glassy blue surface, Elliot could make out the dead body, naked from the waist up.

"Is that your people?" Jackson, the pilot, yelled.

"What people?" Elliot yelled back. Relief floated over him. Relieved that the tanned torso floating face down was a tall, thin, male corpse, and not Ryleigh.

"Your rescue mission?"

Elliot shook his head, not trusting speaking.

"Check him out. We'll need to ID him."

Because of the dense brush around the beach, there wasn't a clean LZ that would allow an easy landing. The chopper dropped low enough that palm trees went thrashing.

After a minute, the pilot lowered the rope over the beach. "Is this good?"

"Yep, I'll radio you when we're ready to go."

"I'm going to rest her over on that island. I'll be close for a few hours." Jackson pointed at the nearest island to the right.

Elliot thought about Operation Puff the Magic Dragon. He thought the fake earthquakes were delayed by a week, but just in case, he replied, "You'd be better off waiting back on the ship."

"I might as well preserve some fuel and take a stroll down the beach. I could use the sunshine. I'll stay close by," he said, pointing in the direction of the nearest island.

Elliot didn't want to argue. He shrugged. "Suit yourself. Be safe."

Elliot wasted no time in getting his gear out of the chopper and onto the island ground safely. His body not even rappelling, but simply sliding down the thick rope like a fireman sliding down a pole, controlling his descent to the soft, sandy beach.

By the time Elliot felt the chopper's wind wake thrusting upwards, he had pulled off his helmet. He looked toward the pilot and held a fist with a thumbs up into the air.

He tugged off his gloves and watched Jackson bank the Sea Hawk back over the clear, blue sea. He removed his heavy boots and replaced them with a pair of climbing shoes from his backpack. He removed his jacket, and underneath he wore an island t-shirt. Ryleigh's favorite.

With the sound of the chopper's propellers droning away, Elliot walked across the beach that was crawling with yellow crabs. He couldn't wait to see her. Would she be happy to see him? Or would she throw a coconut at his head?

He smiled at the warm thought.

He looked up and down the beach; no signs of Ryleigh.

Then he yelled, as he felt the beach beneath him tremble. "No!"

The tremor only lasted a nano-second, but it was followed by another. Then another. And another.

The earthquakes were minor, but they were already starting.

Elliot retrieved his binoculars and scanned the beach, spotting the quiet tiki hut. *Where is Ryleigh?*

He tried to comprehend the sudden, rhythmic, low-toned buzzing that had invaded the beach front. Growing up in Florida, he had never experienced an earthquake. He felt it again. He took off running toward the tiki hut, his mind racing as he ran.

He recalled Dice's report and discussions of a few days earlier. If these were man-made explosions under the earth on the ocean floor, what would that do to the island today?

Elliot made it to the hut, and the empty hammock swung wildly in the stock still air. Thoughts of Ryleigh lying topless in the swing rushed through Elliot. He shook the thoughts and ran toward the hut door.

Inside the hut that had been his and Ryleigh's home for thirty-four days, he found it empty. His blue eyes clouded with tears. He leaned over the handmade quilt of novelty t-shirts, feeling for warmth, but the indentation from Ryleigh's body was cold, and not recently slept in.

He glanced around the hut for any sign of where Ryleigh could have gone. The hunting knife wasn't in its usual place. Wherever Ryleigh had gone, she had the knife. The flashlights were still in their spot, and on impulse he tossed them into his backpack.

He spotted a half coconut with water in it, on the floor of the hut. "So she found the cat."

"Ryleigh!" he yelled.

He stood there a few more seconds and his mind roamed through the last month's warm memories and images there.

Elliot pushed away a tear and the thought that, if Ryleigh wasn't close by waiting for him, it was because she was in danger. But he couldn't stop the feeling that she was hurt or worse. She had to have heard the helicopter land.

She would have made it back to the tiki hut beach by now. Unless...

...Unless she couldn't.

FORTY-SEVEN

BEFORE SEARCHING for Ryleigh, Elliot started a small, controlled fire in the pit, and left a glass, his glass, sitting by the fire. If Ryleigh returned, she would know he was back.

"There's just one more thing I have to do."

Elliot walked back to the tiki hut, wondering where the white island cat he'd left a week ago was at. Was the cat with Ryleigh? Or hiding?

A row of lounge chairs lay on their sides around the hut. *What was she trying to keep out?* Yellow ribbons of lawn chair straps were neatly tied along a palm tree trunk fluttering in the breeze, and as the wind moved across the shore, he could hear the waves splashing. Skeins of sand blew across the beach and built up on the ragged rocks in drifts.

Everything felt familiar. The sounds, the smells, the views. This felt more like home than his condo in Tampa.

He went inside the hut and lifted the straw bed mattress. He threw back the leaves of the small cave floor opening, the dirt safe. It was empty.

"I'll be darned; Ryleigh must be treasure hunting." A boyfriend's pride ran through Elliot at the thought of his protégée not only surviving these last five days alone, but at the image of her hunting.

Elliot zipped along the paths toward the flower hill and the familiar landmarks became visible. He had taken a few minutes to retrieve the body from the sea, so his clothes were wet. The dead man looked like the skipper from the cruise line. His face had been bloated and fish-bitten, but Elliot had been able to make out the features and the portrait of the young man. His name was Trevor.

Elliot had seen plenty of drowning victims, and Trevor hadn't drowned. The body was stiff and it appeared to have died from an arrow shot at close range. The post mortem fish activity had occurred after death

What was the skipper doing back on Keg Key? And who would shoot him and toss him to the sharks?

Racing toward the flower hill and the caves, he saw the tiny island enlarged before his eyes. Seagulls flapped overhead and squawked their welcome back to Elliot.

He hiked for over an hour. Low branches slapped his face and arms, but he raced along, not allowing anything to slow him. He headed in the direction that he and Ryleigh had visited once. The lagoon caves. He had a hunch.

Thank goodness the tremors had settled down in the last hour. But when would they start again? And where was Ryleigh?

His heart raced as he came to a clearing. And that's when he saw her.

"Ryleigh!" Elliot yelled, and ran toward the slumped figure.

She stood up and rubbed her hands over her face as if the bright sunlight was blinding her.

"Thank God you're okay. Baby, I missed you."

Elliot grabbed her and held her close, kissing the top of her head. She squirmed and pushed back.

"Ryleigh, are you okay? Why are you dressed in a leather jacket, and boots?"

She turned her head up, and in a daze, she said, "I'm not Ryleigh. I'm Caleigh."

FORTY-EIGHT

CALEIGH DIDN'T KNOW how long she had wandered in the island fields before the combination of the poison gas and the Taser leads had made her drop headfirst into the sandy soil. Her vision had been blurred and her body had been burning up in her heavy clothes.

She was almost glad for sleep, since it made the dizziness from the cargo plane disappear. The sweet smell of the white alyssums soothed her in and out of sleep. Her legs felt broken from when they had dumped her off the inflatable boat, and from her wandering the island. And someone dragging her. Dropping her down hard.

Her eyes popped open and she sat up, breathing and sweating heavily.

"Elliot," she whispered again at him as he embraced her, squashing her.

She tried to comprehend what Elliot was saying. *What day is it?*

"I can't believe I've been knocked out for almost a day." She did feel bad, but not that sick. Elliot looked at home in his cargo shorts and beat-up, sleeveless t-shirt. He was unshaven and his hair, blonder than it had looked days earlier, was uncombed and shaggy around his face. His blue eyes pierced into her.

"Caleigh Lane, how the hell did you end up here on Keg Key?" He looked around her. "And so quickly?"

"Just hours after you left me, I was kidnapped from the safe house and thrown knocked out on an airplane."

"I did have to take a commercial flight, then a helicopter to the U.S. missile ship, and then we sailed out to these seas and waited for another helicopter ride here. I'll be damned if you didn't make it here before me. And to think Dice has been worried sick about you. Everyone is looking for you." He hugged her again. "I was worried, too."

"Dice?" She felt a curl of fear through her stomach. She hadn't stopped thinking about him for more than a second since she'd been taken. "Where is he? What happened?"

"They infiltrated the compound, catching everyone off guard. The whole night watch, including Dice, was knocked out and tied up."

"Was he hurt?" Caleigh was more worried about Dice, someone she'd known for only a short time, than she was about her own welfare. She should have been shaking and freaking out about being alone on an island, but she wasn't. Was the plan falling apart? Or coming together?

"Not physically. He is in a lot of pain worrying about you."

Caleigh did something she rarely did, and especially with a guy friend; she hugged him. She wrapped her arms around his waist and held on. It didn't matter that he was covered in sweat, sand, and grime; she just held on.

She let go of Elliot, and asked, "Where's Ryleigh?"

"I'm on my way to find her. And you? Why are you here?" Elliot questioned her with his blue eyes. "And let's get you out of these clothes. Did you skydive here?"

"I was Tased, drugged, and– "she winced when she touched her mouth, "–punched."

He looked at her quizzically. "Who did this? Did you see them?" Elliot pulled the jacket off of her shoulders, revealing a tight bodysuit tucked into her jeans.

"No. From the time they pulled me out of the safe house closet, they covered my face and kept me in the dark. I remember a needle in my arm, my head spinning, and then I was out."

Caleigh let a tear slide down her cheek. "I thought I was being drugged and left for dead."

Elliot reached for her hand. He held it while he helped her remove the rest of her leather jacket. "Did you walk all the way here to this field from the tiki hut?"

"You know, I don't remember. I did feel someone dragging me. But it was after they dumped me on the beach. I didn't see the tiki hut. We came in through a boggy coral pass. That, I remember."

"Motorboats can't make it through that pass, without beaching or crashing on the corals. " It was an inflatable. Looked like a canoe. A big orange canoe. Two men and myself. "

"Let me radio Dice and let him know what's going on. I have the helicopter on call, waiting to take us back to the ship. I couldn't fly directly here. That's why it took me so long to get here."

"I didn't see a helicopter." Caleigh looked toward the sky.

"I came here on board a guided-missile cruiser. My buddy, and boatswain's mate seaman Jay Jackson, from Tampa, flew me here on an MH-60S Sea Hawk helicopter. The Hawk was assigned to the Dragon Whale of Sea Combat Squadron 28. After dropping me off, he put her down on that island." Elliot pointed to the largest island in site, on their left. "Just one call and he's back here to take us home."

"Thank God for that. I knew you'd be here."

"But why you? This just doesn't make sense. Why would they want you here, unless– "Elliot looked toward the island.

"Unless, what?" Caleigh's eyes followed his gaze.

"It's an expensive and weak assassination attempt to get rid of you both. You and Ryleigh could be in danger staying here too long."

"But how–," she didn't finish her sentence and her eyes grew wide as she felt the tremor.

They both felt it, at the same time they saw it. Like mini explosions under their feet, and blasts blowing smoke and rock from the neighboring island. The blue sky spurting in the distance with great clouds of fire, surging upwards.

"What the hell is that?" Caleigh fell to the ground, still dizzy from the poisons in her body. "A volcano?"

"Tests. Scientists."

"Nuclear?" The fear of radioactive poisons scared her.

"No. The explosions are meant to be similar to an earthquake. Man-made."

"What? Why?"

"Come on." Elliot grabbed her and pulled her toward the lagoon. "We've got to find Ryleigh. We can hike and I'll explain."

"Do you know where she's at?" Caleigh ran after Elliot, tripping on her boots in the sandy soil paths.

"I'm not certain, but I was thinking the lagoon. She may have found the fresh water springs."

"No, not that way. I think, for time's sake, we want to approach the lagoon from the cliff side," Caleigh said, knowing her sister's life was at stake and that there wasn't much time to explain to Elliot.

Elliot stopped and stared at Caleigh.

"Are you coming?" she insisted.

"Is there something I'm missing?"

"Come on, Elliot, I'll explain soon enough. But I have this gut feeling that my sister is this way. Let's go find Ryleigh."

Caleigh turned toward the lagoon hills, and then they both paused to watch the neighboring island as the dormant volcano became violent just moments after another detonation.

FORTY-NINE

RYLEIGH WOKE UP to a sharp pain across her face.

"Ouch!" She ran her hand across her cheek and felt blood. Was she dreaming? Why did she keep passing out?

She remembered hearing an explosion outside and the cave trembling, the ground shaking, rocks falling off the walls – and that's all she remembered.

Had a rock cut her face?

Something hit her shoulder and, before Ryleigh could draw the knife, she realized a cat had jumped on her neck and was purring madly in her ear.

"Oh my God, Ebba, is that you?"

Ryleigh stroked the matted fur in the dark and scratched behind its ears. "How did you find me?"

The cat was covered with excrement and she smelled awful. Had she entered through the tunnel?

"Okay, I saved your life on this island, and now you're here to save mine."

The cat jumped gratefully into her arms. And swiped at her face. Ryleigh's nose was a constant target for its razor sharp claws.

"Well, hello to you, too," she nuzzled its fur.

"I'm still a dog lover," she whispered into Ebba's fur.

Ryleigh wondered if the faint sounds she had heard earlier had been the cat in the cave.

"How'd you get in here?"

Had Ebba come here before? Maybe she'd been born here. There were plenty of mice and rodents inside the caves to hunt. Ebba had left once for a long time. Could she have walked for hours to get here? Did Ebba chase rodents down the tunnel to the cave?

The pain in her foot was throbbing and it was time to leave the cavern.

"If there was a helicopter earlier, Elliot would be here looking for me. Right?"

"Let's move toward the faint light." Ryleigh squinted toward a small star of light, holding Ebba close and gritting her teeth from the pain, and had moved only a few feet before the ground under her shook.

This time, the earth's movement caused rocks to fall in all directions.

"Shit. This can't be happening! This shipwrecked adventure has got to end."

If this movement kept up, the cave walls could collapse, trapping Ryleigh and Ebba inside forever. The kegs lost once would remain lost. Ryleigh needed to get to an exit fast.

She took a few more steps, and the trembling subsided.

"What is going on?" Ryleigh couldn't recall hearing of earthquakes in this area. But this trembling was enough to register on those earthquake monitors, or what was it Californians called them?

Her mind raced. She couldn't be trapped in rubble. She had already spent what felt like days in the cave.

And then there was Ebba to save.

And there was the treasure.

FIFTY

RYLEIGH!" ELLIOT YELLED again for the fifth time as they approached the lagoon. "Where the hell is she?"

Caleigh sat down and pulled off one boot. She turned it upside down, and shook out a hairbrush. She put her boot back on and zipped it up, tucking the brush into her waistband.

He was about to suggest to her that she shouldn't worry about hair products, when she flashed a weird expression on her face. *Why would she care about her hair?* Both Caleigh and Ryleigh were beautiful women. Now, after spending a few hours with Caleigh alone on the island, he felt he could easily tell the twins apart by their personalities.

There was a rustle in the bushes as they came toward the lagoon.

Caleigh saw it, too.

"Here, take this." Elliot handed her a small leather sheath with a knife. "There are wild hogs on this island and they're probably spooked because of the tremors."

Caleigh placed the knife in her waistband alongside the hairbrush.

Elliot shook his head. "You may want to ditch the hairbrush."

"It's a family heirloom." She winked at Elliot. "My grandmother gave it to me, and her grandmother had given it to her. It's my lucky charm."

There was a mammoth blast, stronger than any of the previous ones they had felt, causing major trembling deep within the earth.

"So you're saying that you think Dexco is behind this?" Caleigh asked, trotting along at his side.

"Yep, we're pretty sure."

"Hmmm," she replied.

Why wasn't Caleigh one bit surprised?

He yelled for Ryleigh again.

Elliot turned around to see that Caleigh had stopped again and was holding her hairbrush.

"Damn it, Caleigh, what are you doing? Are you crazy?"

When she saw him watching, her expression changed. "Just hold on, Elliot. Turn around."

He looked at her, letting her know this was serious. "We don't have time for games."

"Please? I can't explain yet."

Elliot turned his back to the sea. His body signals said, *You've got to be kidding.*

The gorgeous waters he had come to love were now tumultuous. Everything around him was shaky.

"Let's go this way. I have another hunch." Caleigh passed him. "See that cliff? If you can repel down the side, there's an opening in this cave. I just know it. Then it leads to the cavernous waterfall on the other side."

Elliot stopped and reached for her shoulder. He turned her toward him. "Caleigh, why do you think you know all this?"

"Elliot, you have to trust me. I heard things on the plane coming over here."

"Dexco? How would they know about the island and where Ryleigh's located?" He was running out of ideas. They had searched a few of the beaches when they'd flown over them hours ago, and he'd thought Ryleigh would be standing there, waving her hands.

"Okay, let's check it out. But there's no guarantee Ryleigh's in that cave."

"Trust me, the caves are the last place I want to be. But I heard the men talking about it. I'm passionate about this being the only place that makes sense. It's risky, I know. But almost 100% certain she's there. You have to trust me."

"With the explosions, this would be a last-ditch option."

"You told me earlier that you were stuck in these caves when you went to the lagoon and swam in. Right?"

"Yes, the high tides came in and I was stuck there all day. Ryleigh was livid. It was a few weeks ago. The tide patterns would be different now."

"But it's the only thing that makes sense. Where else can she be? There's nowhere else she could be on this island. Unless she's gone."

They were silent in their own thoughts for a few minutes.

"I have to admit, the tiki hut looked like she was planning to return," Elliot said quietly.

"Then let's check out the cave. Sooner the better, before the next explosions occurs," Caleigh said.

He was proud of Caleigh. She wore confidence like it was sewn into her panties, and he liked that about a female. Ryleigh was that way, too. But Caleigh was much more determined. It was as if she had a purpose, and she didn't complain. She just wanted to find her sister.

Within twenty minutes, they were at the left side of the cliffs that led to the lagoon and the sea beyond.

Elliot gave in to Caleigh's suggestions to find a small opening on the side of the lagoon cliff. Elliot worked fast, anchoring the rope hook deep into the cave's smooth rock surface. He tested the weight of the set hook by pulling down with the entire weight of his body.

After he was satisfied it was secured, he yelled to Caleigh. She inched her way over the cliff, standing next to him.

"You stay here."

She looked over the side to the thirty feet below, where the rough waves mixed in with a waterfall. Was that a smile Elliot saw on her face?

Caleigh gave him a thumbs-up. She leaned against the cave's cliff ledge.

He made a rope seat, and slowly and in total control, lowered his entire body down to the mouth of the cave.

Within minutes, he saw an opening. Caleigh had been right. But how?

He pushed himself, off the side of the cave wall, like Spiderman repelling down a building, bouncing back and forth a few times until he swung into a hole the size of a Volkswagen, landing on the damp, cold cave floor.

Oddly enough, he saw small footprints. Ryleigh's? He was about to yell her name. He felt her presence, and someone else's. There were two sets of fresh human footprints.

What did the stars have in store for them next?

FIFTY-ONE

IN AND OUT OF consciousness, Ryleigh awoke with a delirious start and a throb in her foot. Her skin felt prickly. The room was pitch dark; all the lights were off. It took her a second to remember where she was. Then she remembered. The island. Alone. The cave.

She thought about calling out. But then she remembered there might be someone else in the cave.

A few thoughts continued to scare her. How she had ended up in the cave was a disturbing puzzle piece. Was it the captain's murderer? Or who else was on the island?

Ryleigh pulled her sore foot toward the small pinhole of light, leaving behind her in the interior of the cave a pitch-black room filled with what had to be kegs.

"Let's go, Eb." She whispered in the dark.

At least the cave's cool interior provided a temporary respite from the searing island heat outside. But Ryleigh was still sweating, and she feared she had a fever from her wounded foot.

And then there was the intruder.

She didn't care anymore. She wanted the hell out of there.

Earlier, she had heard the sound of rotary blades. And explosions? Was Elliot back earlier than planned? And what were the explosions? It had felt like a tremor.

The last place she wanted to be was stuck in a cave near the ocean during an earthquake.

She listened as she slithered forward. Every sound had grown louder in the cave. So had her fear. In the dark cave, each scrape of her bandaged foot across the sandy floor sounded like the full-fledged STOMP of a boot. And each step fueled her panic; what if she was going in the wrong direction? She turned around, and the darkness was immense. She turned back. A dizzying vertigo twisted her sense of direction. It was so confusing in the pitch black with only a pinhole of light.

Ebba clutched at her chest, now tensed up. Ryleigh's head spun around and something glimmered up ahead.

She squinted, and took a few steps forward. As she drew closer, she realized that she was looking at the first light, other than small dots here and there, she had seen in hours, or maybe even days; a beam of faint light rising over her head, on and off.

There it went again. Faint light rays.

Ryleigh's heart rate leapt, and she stumbled forward and fell. *Get a grip, girl! Panic will kill me before the cave gets a chance.*

She squashed her pet, cradling her close. The light in the distance was hope. The walls of darkness had sent terror throughout her body. But the light? What was it? Maybe it was evening outside the cave and the moon was moving over an opening ahead.

She took a deep, labored breath. The dusty cave air was as chalky as an extra strength Tums.

The thought of future riches, and finally stumbling upon the treasure, were ever-so-present in the back of her mind. But so was getting rescued. It was time to get out of the cave. And off of the island. Ryleigh had been alone too long. She had accomplished what she had come here for. The shear excitement of the discovery in the dark cave kept her pain and fear at bay for the moment.

There it was again, and again. The light was getting a tad brighter. *But what was it? Or whom?* She shuffled her feet, as though wiping muddy shoes on a doormat, while the rest of her body remained still.

The intoxicating mix of fear and excitement pumped through her veins. Fear of the unknown lurking around her. Excitement from the discovery surrounding her.

Slowly, she slinked forward, each step wider. She felt his presence. Ryleigh could picture Elliot here. This adventure, the explosions, the light; it all somehow had to be related to him. In the cavernous darkness, she felt Elliot had found her.

A low, half-cry, half-purr escaped Ebba as the cat squirmed and nipped Ryleigh on her ear. Ryleigh withheld a scream, threw open her arms, and Ebba hit the floor.

"Ebba," Ryleigh mumbled under her breath, lowering herself to the ground where the cat had jumped.

"Ebba," she whispered again, but there was no sound in the darkness. Tears welled up at the thought of losing her beloved pet and it gave her a sick feeling in her abdomen.

Ryleigh felt around the ground and crawled on all fours. Her knees scraping the rough surface. She knew how Tom Hanks in *Castaway* had felt when he'd lost Wilson, his only friend, while stranded alone for years.

"Eb," she whispered. A tear slid down her cheek and Ryleigh quickly wiped it away. Standing up, she felt the empty, hollow loneliness. No time for tears.

It had been almost a week since Elliot had left. A horrible, hideous week.

Could it get any worse?

And it did.

A hand closed over her opening mouth. And something sharp dug into her side.

FIFTY-TWO

HE COVERED HER MOUTH.

She panicked.

"Hold still, we don't want to kill you. We want the jewels. We mean business." His voice snarled.

Ryleigh froze, rigid with fear. Prevented from yelling out, it seemed her body was paralyzed. He pulled her against the limestone wall.

The nice thing about the darkness, her assailant couldn't see either. If she could get free, she could pull her knife.

Why didn't he turn on a flashlight? Who means business? Who are they? His authoritarian voice and attitude scared the living hell out of her. *This is my island and my treasure.*

"I'm going to remove my hand." He breathed in her ear. He smelt like he hadn't showered in days. "Don't scream or you'll cause an avalanche. And don't play naive, young lady. You know what I'm looking for."

Ryleigh dug her heels into the soft earth, seeking a foothold in order to make a firm stance. The man grunted at her resistance, jerking Ryleigh forward.

She wrenched her head back, then snapped her teeth shut on his fingers across her mouth.

"You dirty bitch!" he howled.

Before Ryleigh could step away, he slapped her open-handed across the face.

She felt the force and her fingers, out like talons, flashed back. Her untrimmed fingernails raked his face.

He jerked back and stumbled while letting go of her, which gave her just enough time to grab the knife.

She slashed it in the air, catching some part of his arm. She felt the tug of his flesh slice as she whipped the knife wildly.

"You bitch! All we want is the map!"

She opened her throat to scream, but knew that darkness was on her side. She swallowed the scream, controlled her breathing, and squatted low, crawling backwards.

The man was in a blind rage. From the stumbling sounds, he had staggered back. She pictured his blood running out of his stab wound.

Ryleigh wasted no time, and groped the ground for a rock. Blind in the darkness, she collided with a hard surface. Another keg. She shrank down behind it. The swift burst of fear-fed adrenaline had burnt out and was now replaced by sheer terror.

She heard him stagger and heard the distinct sound as he thumbed back a pistol's hammer.

Would he shoot in the dark?

"If you shoot a gun in here, it will cause an avalanche. We'll be buried alive." Ryleigh prayed he was alone. He had said, *we mean business.*

"Give me the map."

"Okay. But do you have a light? How can I show you the map?"

"Negative. My partner had one, and he and it dropped down a cliff hole during the first explosion."

Ryleigh looked toward the sound of his voice, trying to make out a silhouette. Could she believe him?

She held her knife in one hand and a small handful of pebbles in the other. She threw the handful to her left.

It all happened so fast.

The gun-bearing treasure-hunter turned at the sound and fired his gun, twice. The explosion of his gun was overwhelmed by the sound of explosions overhead, and the sounds of rushing water.

"Look what you've done."

Ryleigh remained silent and perfectly still.

"You and your lying sister think you know everything."

He was moving closer to her. Why had he brought up Caleigh? But she couldn't talk or even breathe. He was so close she could smell him. And, there was his gun.

Several silent minutes later, he had closed the distance between them, and surprised Ryleigh by shoving the gun in her side. "We're going to work our way out of here and you'll give me the map."

Why did he want the map? How had she gotten here? He had to have brought her to the cave. He wouldn't kill her, if he still didn't know where the treasure was.

At the moment, though it was totally illogical and probably not a smart idea, she started laughing.

He shoved the butt of the gun deeper into her side, causing her to grunt from the pain, but it still didn't stop the laughter.

"Of course," she said between laughs.

"What is your problem?" he asked, poking her again with the gun.

Before Ryleigh could answer, she heard the crunching sound of feet behind them.

The man pulled her closer, whispering in her ear, "One word and I swear I'll pull this trigger."

Ryleigh chewed on her bottom lip. She quickly realized that a happy trigger finger could put a bullet in her at close range. And now she had Caleigh to think about, and to tell about the treasure, and she couldn't do that if she was dead.

FIFTY-THREE

RYLEIGH'S HANDS were shaking so violently that she had trouble reaching for her knife.

She heard a popping explosion, a rushing bullet sound echoing in the cave. She fell to the floor.

How many Jenga pieces can you pull and keep the cave from collapsing?

Bullets ricocheted above her head, and she clamped her hands over her ears. Something or someone heavy fell on her, forcing the breath from her body.

A second later, it was quiet and the weight was removed. Ryleigh lay motionless, trying to get both her brain and her body to function normally.

"Ryleigh?" Her name was an urgent whisper.

Rolling onto her side, she saw a flashlight come on, and the bright light burned her eyes. She looked into Elliot's worried eyes behind his night-vision goggles.

"You okay?"

She blinked and nodded as he lifted her into his arms.

"What took you so long?" she asked, wrapping her arms around his neck and collapsing as if she were a puppet whose strings were cut.

Elliot smiled by the glow of the flashlight.

"We'll talk about it later." He brushed some stray strands of hair from her tear-stained cheeks. "I'm so glad you're all right. I can't tell you how frantic I've been, looking for you."

"You've been looking for me?"

"Always," he said, just before his mouth claimed hers.

Ryleigh had been limping her way forward for ten minutes. Elliot had the flashlight in one hand and her arm over his shoulder, assisting her.

"So the night vision goggles came in pretty handy here."

"Perfect aim, he didn't know it was coming." He handed her the canteen.

"How'd you know I was here?" She drank like a camel.

"I'll explain in a minute. Let's get out of here."

"Who was he? He said he had a partner that fell off the cliff?"

"Yes, they came here by the rocky coral side."

Ryleigh let out a small yelp as her sore foot tripped up. "I can't leave without Ebba."

"Who?"

"My feral cat. I found her the day after you left."

Elliot smiled. "You found a pet? Don't worry. I'll find it. We need to get you out of here before another tremor." Elliot grasped her closer. "We're almost there."

It was true. Ryleigh could now make out the light coming from the hole at the side of the cave. It was daylight.

Her eyes burned and stung as they slowly adjusted to the bright light as they made their way through a small opening and out onto a ledge. "I can't leave her behind," she choked out a small whisper. Blinking at the bright sunlight, she rubbed her eyes.

"It will be okay."

"There's a narrow tunnel that leads to the hillside. Do you think Ebba can get out through the tunnel?"

"She'll probably go out the way she got in." Elliot wasted no time; he strapped Ryleigh into a rope seat.

She glanced over the side of the narrow rock shelf they were on. "Oh my, how did I get here?" She could see a turquoise drop of solid rocks and waterfall below, cascading into the rough sea.

"Low tide. Another entrance," Elliot gasped between tugging on the rope that hung from on top of the mountain and ended at the opening. "We came in the cliff side. The other entrance is by the lagoon. You can enter under the waterfall."

"By the lagoon?"

"Yes. Under the lagoon. Two different ways into the caves. As the hill descends, it spills into a lagoon. If you can swim under the waterfall, you can enter the cave from ground level. If you can't swim, you have to climb these rocks and propel down through this opening. The lattice work of caves runs all over these islands."

"Several entrances? That makes sense. "

"Even though the cave was dark, with my night goggles, I could see the underground was a catacomb of holes and cervices. A good swimmer could get to the caves by using scuba gear or holding their breath, but I don't know about the tunnel, other than the cliff side I came through."

"Entrance from the lagoon?" That would explain her wet clothes. But it didn't explain how she had gotten there. To drag a semi-conscious person was a risky move, and considering swimming underwater while pulling a body was a bad idea, and someone could end up dead.

Who could hold their breath that long? And risk drowning Ryleigh? She knew only one person with that talent, and they shared the same DNA.

Everything made sense.

"I'm going to climb up the side to the top. Then I'll pull you up on this seat."

"Are you sure this can hold me? I can't climb myself because of my foot."

"I know. It's okay. I tested it with my weight." Elliot looked up.

Ryleigh's eyes followed his, and for a minute she thought she saw another hand above them. A small, black, gloved hand. Then it was out of sight.

Ryleigh felt herself smile. In that instance, she perceived an unexpected truth about their predicament, one she would verify in the next few minutes.

She felt the sun hot on her neck. "Let's do this."

Elliot leaned over and kissed Ryleigh's forehead. "See you at the top."

She watched him ascend the side of the grotto. Her eyes watched for a few moments and then trailed back to the cavernous opening. A cool breeze radiated from the cave. She smiled.

X marks the spot, with a dot, dot, dot and a dash, dash, dash, and a big question mark. And a pinch and a squeeze and a cool tropical breeze....

...the water trickles up, the water trickles down, and the water trickles all around. Crack!

FIFTY-FOUR

CALEIGH SAT NEXT to the fat coil of rope tied at the base of the palm tree, waiting for Elliot to emerge.

Her gloved fingers clenching and relaxing. Clenching, relaxing. Her hands were sweating so badly under her gloves, but she wanted to wear them in case he needed her to pull on the grizzled rope to help Ryleigh up.

After a few moments of staring at the rope, his hand came over the top and rested before pulling himself over the ledge.

Elliot rolled over and, without looking at Caleigh, he yelled back over the side. "I'm going to pull you up! Use your good leg and arms to keep from hitting the sides!"

"Okay! Got it!"

Caleigh heard her sister yell from below.

Elliot then turned around. "You need to make sure my rope stays taut."

"Okay. She's a bean stalk. We can do this." Caleigh pulled the rope wrapped around Elliot's waist and made sure it was taut before securing a boat knot around the tree trunk. If Ryleigh fell, she'd have to take Elliot and the palm tree with her.

Elliot began to pull, his tanned triceps flexing with each loop of the rope he threw behind him. Caleigh gathered the excess rope and wrapped it around the tree. The fact that she could not look over the edge and see Ryleigh, in fear of startling her into a horrible descent, made the roping process more arduous.

Elliot shifted his stance and his boots slipped in the sandy soil.

All of Caleigh's senses wired to the cliff's edge as Elliot caught his footing.

He looked behind him, mutely nodding.

He made three more pulls, and Caleigh made three more loops around the tree. Pull. Loop. Pull. Loop. Pull. Loop.

All of her, every cell, was aching. Not from the physical labor, but for the moment Caleigh would see her twin again. Ryleigh was seconds away from emerging over the cliff's edge and Caleigh couldn't wait to see her. Butterflies filled her insides. Ten years of the two not talking or touching now finally coming to end here on this island.

With one blink, that reunion was put on hold.

FIFTY-FIVE

THE EXPLOSIONS lasted a second, but it was the after-tremor that caused Elliot to slip. The last three loops of the coiled rope went from slack to taut.

Caleigh grabbed the rope tied to his waist, squeezing with both hands, fighting the waves of panic. She had to stop thinking about Elliot sliding to the edge. If they were going to make it through this, she needed to act, not think.

Please, God, help me, she prayed.

She grabbed the rope and wrapped her arms around the tree. And miraculously, it stopped him short of the edge.

"I got it!" he yelled back to Caleigh.

Elliot gave two big tugs and, there before you could save "Eureka," Ryleigh yanked herself up the ledge and landed on Elliot.

Caleigh walked over and looked down at her sister.

Ryleigh looked surprised, or more in shock, but she didn't say anything as she stared up at Caleigh.

It was Caleigh that spoke first. "Didn't they strand you here with a tweezers? You look like you're growing a unibrow."

Ryleigh hobbled up, leaning against Elliot standing behind her. As if she was suddenly aware of her disheveled appearance, Ryleigh attempted to brush sand from her legs, and her hips, and then looked right into Caleigh's eyes. "I never imagined to see you here. But then again, it's starting to all make sense." She smiled.

Caleigh had known that her sister would start to remember once she saw her.

Caleigh hugged her twin sister tightly, frightened by the way she trembled and how small and fragile she felt in her arms. "It's okay, you're safe now. No one is going to hurt you."

Ryleigh hugged Caleigh back, and started rambling. "I knew it was you! I felt it. You saved my life. I missed you!"

Elliot, with a puzzled look, said, "Oh really?" He pulled Ryleigh into his arms and hugged her tightly, too. "Who saved your life? Technically, I found you in the cave."

"No, I found her. Because I'm the one who dragged her skinny ass to the lagoon and practically drowned her to get her into the cave," Caleigh said.

"What? Can someone please explain to me why you two aren't surprised to see each other?"

Caleigh and Ryleigh looked at each other eye to eye.

Elliot grabbed Ryleigh's hand. "Ryleigh, remember, no more lies. This island is no longer about secrets and lies."

Caleigh knew it was time for some truths. "I was the one that saved Ryleigh from the two men."

"What? But how?" Elliot's eyes went from Ryleigh, standing there and nodding her head, to Caleigh, smiling back in admiration.

Tears were flowing down both of their faces.

"I missed you," Ryleigh whispered. Her eyes were damp with tears. She mouthed to Caleigh, *it's okay. You can tell him. We can trust him.*

"They brought me here, hoping I'd give them the map. Or lead them to the treasure," Caleigh said.

"Who?" Elliot's questioning eyes went from Caleigh to Ryleigh.

"Greg's guys," Caleigh said.

The twins' tears fell in earnest now. The two of them stood together for the first time in a long time.

"Greg, the CEO of Dexco Pharmaceuticals?" Elliot asked.

"Yes," said Ryleigh, brushing away a tear.

"And the murderer of our parents," added Caleigh.

FIFTY-SIX

RYLEIGH HAD NEVER dreamed for one second that she would be the one to have hidden lies and secrets from Elliot Finn, the master intelligence guru that he was. The sun lowering into the sea framed his tall silhouette, outlining the slump in his otherwise broad shoulders. The magnificent blue waters in the background.

Oh, how she had missed her Hunk-a-berry Finn. His dirty brown hair that waved and molded against his head, as he cocked it to the side looking at her.

"Okay. Okay. Slow down. I think I heard you wrong." He wore her favorite island t-shirt, which hadn't gone unnoticed by Ryleigh. *Good choice, Hunk-a-berry.*

"No, Elliot, you heard Caleigh right."

"But your parents died in a car wreck."

"Yes, they did. Technically, they did have an accident by running off an icy road. Case closed. But we found out why they ran off the road later on. After we hired a detective," Ryleigh said.

"After we opened the safety deposit boxes," Caleigh chimed in.

"What safety deposit boxes?" Elliot's voice was devoid of any hint of recognition of the past.

Ryleigh had thought he may have figured some of it out. "Our parents. We got the keys to the boxes when we turned 21. They left us a lot of information. About treasure hunting. And a sealed letter."

Ryleigh stared into his cobalt blue eyes.

He met her stare with one equally as steady. "What did it say?"

"It said, if they were ever found dead together by an unexplainable circumstance, like a house fire, or random shooting, or anything not of natural causes, that we should call a detective named Chandler and hire him to explore the cause of their deaths. They said that further analysis might point to Greg Edersom's, well, Greg's grandfather, William Edersom Brown."

"Captain Ed Brown?" Elliot asked.

It was Ryleigh's turn to have a surprised look on her face. "Yes."

"The Captain of Illyria? Hidden treasures in Cocos Islands?" He smiled at Ryleigh, a dawning expression on his face. "And here I thought you were cruising along these rugged shorelines, collecting shells, hermit crabs, and sand dollars."

She remembered how, over a week ago, she had let him leave the island and had pressed a sand dollar into his hand. She had hoped the dollar shell would send some type of recognition.

"I do love shelling. Of course, I was secretly studying the maps, too."

"So how did Greg get involved?"

"His family records. Once he located our family, he wanted to intimidate our parents, and threatened them to find the missing pieces to the unsolved blood diamond treasure."

"Blood diamonds? Like those that African dictators used slaves and children for, to mine the diamonds to sell to fund conflict?"

Ryleigh nodded. "Diamonds were traded to both the east and west. In 1725, some Chinese discovered diamonds and, because of their hardness, it was used to cut jade. Legends had it that a great, great relative of ours rescued a ship carrying stolen diamonds. He buried the diamonds for safekeeping, but died before he could turn them in to the authorities."

"But why your family? Are you related to the De Beers?" Elliot asked, smiling, which quickly turned to a grin when Ryleigh and Caleigh exchanged glances.

"Later. We will get to that later."

"But why here? And Greg?"

"When we got into the safety deposit boxes, we found maps."

"So Greg's family knew our ancestors. And he hired someone to scare my parents, but it backfired. Our dad caught on to it and they tried to outrun them..." Caleigh's voice trailed off.

"He was indirectly responsible for their accident," Elliot acknowledged.

"To us, he might as well have held the smoking gun," Caleigh said.

Ryleigh started talking again, not really to Elliot, but more to Caleigh. "When I graduated, I went to work for them. Most of what I did for Dexco was plotting and procedural. I knew Greg was bad. I just didn't know how much. And the lengths he'd go to for profits. Hurting innocent sick people.

Many late nights, while I was reviewing documents, I set the ball rolling to get Greg Edersom sent away for a long time. I made sure those bad trial studies were found. I entered the studies myself to better catch him."

Caleigh walked over and slipped her arm around Ryleigh's waist. "It's okay, we'll get him."

"He's a murderer. He'd do anything in an effort to prevent me or anyone from publicizing the details of a botched trial of their hot, new drug that's for the treatment of diabetes that has resulted in the deaths of many of the subjects."

Ryleigh kept talking, "Greg's obsessed about finding the treasure. In his sick mind, he thinks it's his. And he's using blood money to do his research and explorations. Now, ten years later, all these maps converged, and they all meet here at the crossroads. And he's still after us."

"Do the maps end here?" Elliot asked.

"We weren't sure. And, well, if Caleigh hadn't been here to carry me out of the flower field to safety, Greg's hatchet men would have finished me off, after they stole my map."

Elliot turned to Caleigh. "You knew about these caves?"

"I've been waiting ten years to be here." Caleigh said.

FIFTY-SEVEN

THE THREE OF THEM traversed the now trampled path.

Elliot stopped and retrieved a blue Humalog KwikPen of insulin from his backpack. "It's been in the cooler except for the last few hours," he said, handing it to Ryleigh.

Ryleigh's eyes were moist. "You knew?" As she removed the insulin needle's cap, her eyes shifted from Elliot to Caleigh.

"We do." Caleigh gave Ryleigh a squeeze.

"You met my endocrinologist?" she asked as her practiced hands carefully inserted the needle in her thigh.

"I met your entire diabetes team," Elliot said. "You should have told me. We have had some serious trust issues."

"I did let you strand us on this island. But plans went terribly wrong. All the lies we told each other. That ends now." Ryleigh felt elated to have Elliot know the truth.

"Let me get this straight. On top of everything else that's happened, you let me strand you here?" Elliot asked Ryleigh.

"First of all, I didn't let you do anything. I had my plans, too, but never expected it to end the way it did."

"I don't understand how Caleigh got involved?"

"She's been superbly trained in all types of treasure hunting."

"Trained?"

"Our grandparents. The last ten years have been tough for me and Caleigh to know something incredibly valuable resided in these caves. We lived quietly, in fear of Greg, hiding this intimate knowledge of our ancestor's history. Waiting for the right moment."

"Now I do have some catching up to do," Elliot said. "And you won't have to worry about Greg Edersom anymore. Seems he's going to be behind bars for a long time."

"Because of Dexco's diabetes drug deaths?"

"Yes, he'll have to deal with those charges, but right now he's in jail because he's somehow connected to a dead detective, amongst a few other charges."

"Greg killed a detective?" Caleigh asked. "Oh my God, not Chandler?"

Elliot nodded. "Not with his own hands, but through one of his men. So, now there's a dead detective I'll have to deal with when I return to the States. That just makes my job a lot tougher."

"Well, you have a body in the caves we have to deal with, too," Ryleigh reminded him. She had stopped and turned back toward the cliff's edge, and sat down on a rock. Her foot was aching so badly she wanted to scream.

Caleigh looked at Ryleigh when she mentioned the caves.

"Speaking of bodies, who did the dead skipper work for?" Elliot asked the two sisters.

"Trevor? I assumed he was a local treasurer hunter that got in Greg's way. Or maybe another treasure hunter went after him. We'll leave that homicide for the local police."

"By the way, does Dice know about Greg? And is Dice going to meet us?" Caleigh asked.

"Who's Dice?" Ryleigh asked.

Elliot looked at Caleigh. "He's fine. A little bruised ego-wise, but he'll be fine."

Ryleigh raised her eyebrows and looked over at Caleigh. She saw a sparkle in her twin's eyes.

Caleigh shrugged and smiled. She walked over and placed Ryleigh's arm around her shoulder, and Elliot took Ryleigh's other arm. Both lifted her.

"We have a lot of catching up to do, sis," Caleigh said.

"I can hobble a little, but we can't leave without Ebba."

"Who's Ebba?" Caleigh asked.

Just then, a small tremor came from under their feet. The ground shifted, and they watched as rocks tumbled down the hill and splashed into the ocean.

"Ladies, I'd love for us to stay and chat, but we need to get the hell out of here, and fast."

"How are we leaving? What's the plan?" Caleigh asked Elliot.

"He's the top chief of intelligence for the agency. Isn't that right, Elliot? Why don't you get on the radio you have hidden in your cargo shorts and call for back-up?"

"Well, here's the problem. When my rope slipped earlier, and I flipped upside down trying to save my life, it fell out of my pocket. It now sits at the bottom of the sea."

Two more explosions erupted within seconds of each other.

"This plan is going to hell in a handbasket," Caleigh said.

Ryleigh stopped and wiggled free from Caleigh's grasp. "All you really cared about was the treasures, anyway."

"Do you mean right before you tricked Elliot into leaving you here on the island, you didn't care about finding the treasures? Look where that's left us. Stranded on an exploding island, alone, with no back-up, or a radio. And no treasures, and looking for someone you call Ebba." Caleigh was raising her voice with each word.

Ryleigh reached down, pulling off her makeshift bandage, her yellow bandana. She'd had enough of the hard, prickly shards in the fabric. While she was playing with her foot, the white island cat wandered between her feet. Ryleigh grabbed her and stood up.

"Meet Ebba." Smelling like the foul odor of the small tunnel, Ryleigh realized Ebba must have worked her way to the hillside though the tube she had tried to crawl through earlier.

"Okay, so can we go now, ladies?" Elliot asked.

"Before we rush off, I want to show you something," Ryleigh said. "But first, Caleigh, show me the map."

"What?" Caleigh looked hurt and curious at the same time.

"Come on. I know you have it." Ryleigh winked at Elliot, who now stood with his hands on his hips.

"Ladies, this is crazy. It's all legends."

"Caleigh, show him." Ryleigh moved closer to her twin. The fire inside her was still burning with excitement.

"Where's yours?" Caleigh asked.

"The bad guys took it. But not before I found something." She moved closer to lean on Elliot.

"Okay, okay." Caleigh reached into her belt and pulled out the silver hairbrush.

"You're going to brush your hair again?" Elliot questioned Caleigh.

Caleigh unscrewed the top of the brush and snapped it open. She turned the cylinder part of the brush's handle upside down and shook out a rolled piece of paper.

Ryleigh smiled. "Grandma's brush." She saw Elliot's bright sea blue eyes blinking at them.

"Yep. My talisman. My good-luck charm."

Ryleigh reached for the faded paper. She rolled it open. It was crude and sparse, but it was identical to her map. Right down to the ink smudges. She recognized the points of reference – there was the spherical shape on the map that looked like it had a tail.

"This is where we're at," Ryleigh said, pointing to a spot that had been so familiar to her. "And this is where I was hiding. I found the kegs."

Elliot shook his head. "They're empty. Old whiskey barrels, found throughout these islands."

Caleigh's expression deflated.

"Yes, they are empty, and they once held wine or modern-day whiskey. Now, their sealed lining is decrepit, falling apart. And their metal rims are rusted."

Caleigh cocked her head; the grin she flashed was the one from their youth.

Without saying a word, Elliot pulled the water canteen out of his backpack, took a swig, and handed it to Ryleigh. Ryleigh took a long gulp of the water and handed it to Caleigh.

Wiping water from her lips, Ryleigh said, "Have you ever heard of lining barrels with clay or glass?" Her foot throbbed, but even though she was battered and bruised, she felt blissful. Her dream was coming true.

"The types of barrels or kegs we're talking about are unlike the rest of the modern day wine storage devices. These kveri kegs were the first to be used, and then later the amphorae storage devices were designed to be kept in the ground to ensure climate control in Italy. These storage devices were the ancient way to transport wine, olive oil, other prized liquids. Our ancestor used them to smuggle items inside some of the wine jugs."

She glanced at Elliot, and grinned and winked at Caleigh.

FIFTY-EIGHT

RYLEIGH HAD THE FLOOR, and Caleigh and Elliot listened with rapt interest.

"I guess they used these types of kegs to preserve the liquor, for the men at sea, and the long journeys across the vast oceans," Elliot said.

"Yes, for a long time, the amphorae were the way the majority of wine was shipped over long distances throughout empires."

"I've read of recent shipwrecks throughout the Mediterranean that revealed that wine was often transported in these large containers." Elliot's eyes were lit up with excitement. "Few people even think about the fact that wine crossed a country or an ocean in a monstrous wooden vat."

"Not our ancestors," Caleigh chimed in.

"It's true. Our family history tree, our great, great, great grandfather was the only child of a wine merchant, and inherited a huge fortune. He bought ships, and was an active seaman that transported wine and jewels to royalty around the world. Many ships transporting expensive cargo were lost to sea, and a few taken by pirates, as crew would defend themselves desperately and never surrender."

Elliot waited quietly.

"Well, I guess one of our great grandfathers was a bit of a scoundrel and got interested in treasure-hunting business along the way. He hooked up the wrong captain and rumor had it that they stole a king's treasure for his daughter. Of course, this is all a legend."

"What makes you two think the treasure is here?"

"I don't *think* it is here. I know it's here."

"Ryleigh, sweetheart, how can you be so certain that the key to all this lay quietly here waiting in the tropical seas of the South Pacific– "

"Well, a barrel broke inside when I fell on it. I thought I'd cut my foot on the glass." Ryleigh smiled. "See if this doesn't change your mind about rushing off the island."

She opened the yellow bandana pouch, pouring the contents into her hand and smiling broadly into the sunshine. Small and large crystal rocks sparkled in the crux of her palm.

Elliot studied the treasured diamonds.

Ryleigh's heart thumped and he laughed.

"After years of our ancestors searching this atoll of islands, these caves were hidden by tides and scoured by hurricanes, and the sea transfigured the landscape, making the maps near impossible for an amateur."

Ryleigh's joy plunged her back into their childhood memories… their parents' relentless travels around the world on antique jewelry shopping expeditions. They weren't shopping, like they led most people to believe, they were exploring. They were treasure hunting.

She held out another handful of the shiny, ungroomed rocks. "Great, great grandpa's mining mystery. Diamonds."

"What?" Elliot Finn was speechless.

"The diamonds are historically ours." It was the first time Ryleigh had seen the twinkle in Caleigh's eyes in a long time.

"Caleigh, we found it. I found the motherlode!" she screamed, wrapping her arms around Caleigh. Exhaustion, thirst, tremors, all forgotten.

"You what?" Elliot was still examining the handful of dazzling rocks when Ryleigh launched herself into his arms, sprinkling the sandy path with the precious stones.

"I thought I was going to faint when I felt the jewels. And I tasted them – and the way they clanked against my teeth, the hardest known material, I knew. I just knew."

Ryleigh talked nonstop, recounting every second of her discovery in the cave. She swung around in a one-legged, whirly dance and grabbed Elliot's hand. Then she reached for Caleigh's and linked the three of them together.

FIFTY-NINE

ELLIOT HAD KNOWN the moment he had met Ryleigh Lane that she held a unique secret.

"This explains why Greg has hired the scientists to cause the explosions around these islands. They're mining. All this time, legends were that the treasures were buried on the island somewhere."

"When I heard about the Royal Cruise line sailing here to this area, I booked my ticket. And then I met you, Hunk-a-berry Finn. I just needed you to throw off Greg Edersom," Ryleigh said.

"I never thought you'd find the treasures without me." He lifted her hand and pressed his lips to her knuckles.

"Without you..." She pulled her hand from his.

He could read the concern, the regret, and painfully, the curiosity in her eyes. "I looked for it, too."

"You knew about the maps?"

"I had my suspicions."

"How much did you know?" Ryleigh's brow creased.

"I knew a lot." Elliot thought he would tell her soon about how much he had discovered about her and her family's history. He knew that one day he'd even tell her about Greg and how he knew what this nasty guy's intentions were. He'd known that Greg would never stop searching for the diamonds. He'd known that eventually Greg would have been done using the Lane girls and their family, and toss them aside like he had their parents. But he couldn't tell her yet. They needed more time to trust each other again.

"We can talk about that later. Right now – bring me those lips again." Elliot pulled Ryleigh to his side and pressed his lips on hers.

"I hate to break up you two lovebirds, but we still have a big problem; without the radio, how do we plan to get off this island?" Caleigh asked.

"She's right, I lost the radio. We have no way to call the helicopter but, we can take the inflatable canoe on the coral side to where the chopper is set down. The Dexco guys left it on the other side of Keg Key." The treasures, Elliot decided, would need a private vessel. He needed to get to a radio and make the call to the person he trusted the most in matters like this, Dice.

"Of course."

"But first I need to climb down that cliff wall and mark the caves and the kegs. I need to do it quickly before another explosion and the entrances get buried. Markers need to be set for when we return. Will you two wait while I grab my backpack?"

Caleigh and Ryleigh exchanged a glance. "Only if Caleigh goes with you this time and helps."

"Seriously, you don't trust me now, after all we've been through?" He winced.

"It's not about trust. It's about who finds the treasure and recovers it." Ryleigh laughed and threw her arms around him. "Oh, Elliot, this is it. I just know it."

Elliot winked at Caleigh, and then jerked his thumb toward the cliff. "Whenever you're ready, Ms. Lane and Ms. Lane. We need to set the markers."

"And grab some of our treasures," Caleigh said.

"Let's hurry, so we can get Ryleigh to the ship to have her foot looked at."

Ten minutes later, Ryleigh watched Caleigh and Elliot, the two people she cared the most about in the world, descend down the cliff side of Keg Key.

It made her nervous to realize the she'd been singled out by Greg for other reasons besides the pharmaceutical trial, but she smiled to herself. They had finally won.

She thought about Caleigh and how she'd been alone in her world, all these years. Caleigh was up in her head now, cool as cool, trying to collate the sentimentalities they had shared. Only like twins could do. They were one again.

As Elliot and Caleigh scaled the cliff, she heard them chatting.

"In our family growing up, it wasn't about golf, tennis or other sports, it was always about treasure hunting. Our parents taught us that. We were weaned on the hunt. Many years later, Ryleigh and I made a plan."

"Was this part of your plan?"

"Yes, we came to these islands when we were young. But over the years, these islands have changed; mostly, I think for the better."

"I wish I could say that about the rest of the world..."

Ryleigh let out a deep, relaxed sigh, and squeezed Ebba, pressing the scrawny cat to her neck.

"We did it, Ebba," she whispered. "We did it."

X marks the spot, with a dot, dot, dot and a dash, dash, dash, and a big question mark. And a pinch and a squeeze and a cool tropical breeze.

EPILOGUE

WHEN THEY WERE brought back to the docks, and Ryleigh saw solid land with cars, their rescue finally sank in. She began to feel the excitement in the air.

The navy ship lay at anchor in deeper water, surrounded by a flock of buzzing watercraft filled with people who'd heard of the news. The water was furrowed with the wakes of motor boats, jet skis and even inflatables. Cell phones buzzed. Walkie-talkies honked. Cameras clicked. Their rescue was the hottest trending social media story. Detectives, police, coastguard personnel, and reporters stood among the hundreds of onlookers on the boat docks.

Ryleigh cradled a handheld walk-talkie, turned low to communicate with Caleigh. Caleigh had a devout wish that nobody would pay any attention to her. She hated reporters. Dice had taken her twin away from the scene already. They felt it was best not to confuse the situation. This was Ryleigh's stranded story. And about her rescue. Caleigh would have her day, when they returned to uncover the treasures.

Ryleigh was below deck, and when she looked out through a porthole, she couldn't believe she saw a large city in front of her. She caught her reflection in the cabin's mirror. Frowning.

What is wrong with me? she asked herself. She'd had a much-needed shower, and her wound tended to, and all the time, Elliot, her Hunk-a-berry, had been at her side. But land was near, and it was time to deal with the reality of what would happen next.

She raked her hands through her hair, wet from the freshwater shower. She felt anxious, seeing land.

Leaving the bathroom, the lights in the ready room of the inner sanction of the squadron were stark white, and bright, despite it being daylight outside. The room was a combination of clubhouse, rest room, and a briefing center. She saw Elliot's glorious body framing the porthole window. They were alone.

Walking toward him, she was aware of her surroundings. The ready room made her feel proud of the U.S. The walls were filled with historic photos and cases filled with trophies, and it felt like a wondrous place. For the first time in months, she felt safe. Safe with Elliot.

He met her eyes, and wrapped an arm around her, imprisoning her. He stared impassively at her with great concern and worry on his face. "Are you okay?"

She nodded, but her body sagged limp like the damp towel in her hand.

"You don't look happy. This is what you wanted, right, Ryleigh? We'll do the press conference and then we'll go back to Chicago. You and Ebba can get settled down, and then we can take it from there."

She shifted, out of his arms, to face him. "I love you. I've had a hell of a time, Elliot. I can wait awhile, but I want the two of you in my life as much as I can get. I want you and Caleigh in my life forever. But I want you to want me. I want you to be mine. I want –"

When she cut herself off, he shook his head. "Say it. You've earned it."

"I want you to be mine, and I don't want to eat another conch or piece of coconut for as long as I live." She smiled, brushing a tear from the corner of her eye.

"You deserve that much. You know what fear is, you do, because you went through it."

"I do know fear. I know what it felt like. And often, I felt a terrible blinding rage burning in me. That fear tangled with rage. That you left me alone. And even knowing what you had to do, I feared I'd never see you again. And that is worse than living alone on the island. The fear that I'd never see you again, or have you hold me at night or take my hand the way you do. So many things, I can't tell you." Tears flowed freely down her cheeks.

"We have a lifetime for you to tell me." Elliot took her hand.

"I knew you'd come back."

He drew a breath. "Of course, I would."

"I wasn't sure. You never really said I love you to me. But I don't care. You're here and you'll get around to it."

He squeezed her hand tighter, and she watched a new look in his eyes. Her heart warmed inside her. "You loved me so easily. I know you didn't trust me, but Ryleigh, you came to love me so easily, and that scared me."

"We both lied a lot. But that's all behind us."

"I'm here, not to complete a mission. I'm here because I love you. I love who you are. I love that you– "

She stepped into him and wrapped her arms around his neck. "I love you too, Elliot. Now grab Ebba and let's do this."

The freshly bathed cat was curled on one of the soft recliners. Elliot picked up her pet, and gave her a genuine, relieved smile.

The ship had come to a complete halt.

"We're here. Are you sure you're ready? You have the script and plan?" Elliot placed his hand in hers.

"Not as ready as I could be. Can we just rest one night at the hotel, after the hospital visit? I don't think I can bear the crowds yet." The tears fell again as the emotions of the last few days mingled with the painkillers from her newly stitched, punctured foot. And now, confirmation that Elliot was all hers.

Elliot reached out and hugged her as close as he could, wiping tears from her face. "We will spend the night in peace. The press conference can wait."

She sniffled. "Thank you."

He kissed her gently on her suntanned cheek. And when she started to speak, he kissed her again, deeply. "I love you, Ryleigh Lane."

"That makes everything all better," she said as she pulled him into her. "I love you, too."

The first night in the hotel, Ryleigh was so exhausted, she slept as if dead. She had not seen solid shelter over her head or had a soft mattress to lie upon in forty-five days.

That evening, after their hospital health check-up, they were escorted to the Grand Hotel ballroom, where TV camera crews were set up.

At the press conference, they said they were both stranded, and that Elliot had made it off the island first and come back for her. Dice and the bureau had it all worked out.

Ryleigh and Elliot carefully answered the press questions.

An elderly lady asked, "Could you have tolerated a longer stay?"

"Yes." But then Ryleigh quickly added, "but not much longer."

A young man asked if she'd had nightmares. *Boy, had she.*

A female reporter that looked to be in her twenties asked if life on the island alone had brought them closer to each other. Ryleigh smiled and wrapped her arm in Elliot's.

"That's irrelevant," Elliot said into the mike.

They answered questions for twenty minutes. Someone asked if they would be suing the cruise ship company. "The thought never occurred to me," Ryleigh answered honestly.

A reporter asked, "What's the first thing you two want to do when you return to the States?"

Both felt that a rest, as far from the water as possible, was in order. Maybe a walk in the country or a mountainside spa resort where they could be pampered and waited on and eat junk food. And return for the treasure as soon as possible, she thought. Her fingers rubbing the smooth stone in her jean pocket.

When asked what they'd missed most, Ryleigh replied, "Chocolate, ice cream, books, and my bed."

On the third day, after the longest bath of her life, Ryleigh ate a soul-surviving, nourishing breakfast. She was still stuffed from all the room service she had eaten the night before.

She and Caleigh had spoken a little about the last fifteen years, trying to fill in some of what Ryleigh referred to as the lost years.

But mostly Ryleigh felt an aching to return to her discovery on the island, as soon as they could. It was all hers and Caleigh's, and now Elliot's. She wanted to explore new possibilities with him. After what they'd survived, nothing could stand in the way of their happy life together. Nothing.

NINE THOUSAND, EIGHT HUNDRED and fifty-two miles away from Ryleigh and Elliot, in a Chicago prison, Greg Edersom cursed under his breath. When he had learned he was under criminal investigation by the FBI last year, the Dexco Pharmaceuticals CEO should have kept a low profile. But no, instead, he'd gone to Keg Key months ago — and had kept himself occupied with his crazy notion of blowing his way through the island atolls, looking for the lost treasures. He'd had his team spend the last few months excavating the islands and their caves.

Greg crumpled a bathroom tissue and slam-dunked it into the trash can.

The fact that Greg was faking the island explosions as a way to mine for the treasures was an easy scam. His blackmail scheme against several high-end officials guaranteed his scientists would continue to test out the gases and their effects in the islands. In the U.S, the exploration violations would have drawn hefty fines, but in the South Pacific Seas, bribing their government officials was easier, though still a felony punishable by time in prison. But he felt he would never be caught.

Then the drug trial had hit the media spotlight for months, delaying his exploration. With the expedition put on hold, he risked other treasure hunters discovering the treasures. And all because of that Ryleigh bitch. His tongue darted out to lick his lips. "It should be all mine."

Feeling trapped like a rat in a snake's mouth, he waited impatiently for his legal team to bail him out. Greg had been arrested for criminal and civil actions after a routine traffic stop had effectively waved a red flag. That red flag had turned out to be a dead ex-cop in the back of the van he was driving. Of course, the vehicle hadn't been his and he would be cleared, but he had a mess to clean up. "They'll never convict me. This is a slam dunk. No eyewitnesses, no motive."

He looked around, his eyes locked on the camera in the corner of the holding cell. "They can't hold me liable. I've known for months that the bureau has been keeping an eye on me and my company."

He wadded up another tissue, and made a basketball move,

tossing the paper wad at a trash can. It landed on the floor next to a half a dozen other balled-up tissue clumps. Trials in Chicago where celebrities were involved were fairly predictable. Especially if the defendant was as good as Greg on the witness stand. The jury would buy his act. He felt confident that he would stroll out of the courtroom scot free.

He tore off another toilet tissue and began rolling it into a ball. "It's preposterous and crap. Many pharmaceutical companies are repeatedly found guilty of fraud, cover-ups of fatal side effects, and for paying huge kickbacks to doctors, and manipulating scientific research. And everyone gets away with it. And I will, too. Soon I'll be free. Off the hook. Cruising the islands."

He threw another paper wad at the basket. It hit dead center in the can. "Two points! Big pharma gets away with murder. And I will soon be free. Then the treasures will be mine to discover. All mine."

Nothing will get in my way. Nothing.

ABOUT THE AUTHOR

Pamela Laux Moll

Pamela Laux Moll loves traveling and attributes her creative inspiration to it. Many of her adventures are to remote tropical islands. She lives on an island near Saint Petersburg, Florida.

Pamela has published several catalogs, calendars, guide books, and novels.

I hope you enjoyed Book Two of the Survival Island Suspense Series! Your feedback is important to me and inspires me.

If you liked Book Two: *Girl Alone on an Island,* please go to www.gopamela.com and register to be the first to receive Book 3 in the trilogy: Diamond Island Available Fall 2016. Get on the list to Pre-Order Book 3 and win an Amazon Gift Card:

www.gopamela.com

In the meantime, if you liked this and other stories by Pamela, please go to where you bought it, and write a review, so other readers can hear from you.

Or leave a review on Goodreads or Amazon. Thanks for reading!

https://www.amazon.com/Island-Lies-Survival-Suspense-Book-ebook/dp/B018Y0PS0Y/ref=sr_1_1?ie=UTF8&qid=1467028709&sr=8-1&keywords=island+of+lies

BOOKS by Pamela Laux Moll

Plush	Published 2012
Island of Lies	Survival Island Suspense Series Book One
Girl Alone on an Island	Survival Island Suspense Series Book Two
Diamond Island	Survival Island Suspense Series - Fall 2016 Book Three
SUE ME	A retread of Plush - Summer 2016
Billet	A Hockey Mom's Story - 2017

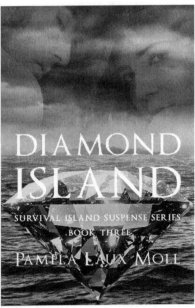

Two survivors. One island. No one to trust...

Ryleigh Lane desperately needed a vacation. The whistle-blower is about to appear in court to go up against a corrupt pharmaceutical exec. If she's successful, the case will reveal a deadly secret. Shortly before the trial, a carefree cruise with her new boyfriend, Elliot, changes everything. A sudden storm leaves them stranded alone on a tiny island.

Elliot Finn is incredibly mysterious... and completely sexy. His resourcefulness helps Ryleigh get through the early days on the island. But as they fight for survival, Ryleigh realizes they're both guarding dark secrets.

Romance blooms alongside suspicion. Will this new case put Ryleigh's life on the line?

Island of Lies is the first book in the Survival Island series, a set of suspenseful thriller novels. If you like sizzling chemistry, riveting suspense, and twists you won't see coming, then you'll love Pamela Laux Moll's captivating series starter.

Buy *Island of Lies* to journey to the island today!

A collectables craze. A deadly secret. Only one woman is willing to fight back.

Sue Logan will do anything for her family. The single mom's startup is her best chance for earning a living, but a secret she learns along the way might put her and her bank account out of business. Everyone Sue knows is obsessed with collecting an extremely popular plush toy. Except the toy could be deadly, and Sue may be the only one who realizes it...

When a billionaire toy manufacturer tries to run Sue out of business, she enlists the help of a shady journalist to save herself and her children. But can Sue trust the reporter long enough to outwit the corporate giant before the unthinkable happens?

Sue Me is a legal suspense thriller. If you like fast-paced drama, strong female characters, and the movie Erin Brockovich, then you'll love this refreshing debut novel from Pamela Laux Moll.

Buy *Sue Me* to collect your next read today!

Previously Published as Plush.

36783643R00154

Made in the USA
San Bernardino, CA
03 August 2016